SCANDALS IN SAVANNAH

THE SOUTHERN SLEUTH BOOK 2

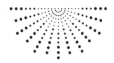

HARPER LIN

ISBN: 978-1-987859-74-4

www.harperlin.com

CHAPTER ONE

SAVANNAH, GEORGIA, 1922

*B*ecky Mackenzie looked out the window as she sat in the red velvet armchair in the family sitting room. She admired the pretty colors of the leaves, because soon they would be gone when the cooler months came. Absently, she played with the long string of pearls she wore with her new dress. Mama said the dress was rather garish with the waist dropped so low but with the hem higher than she approved of. Becky told her all the flappers were wearing it. That sent her mother into a tizzy that would have scared every German back to Germany in the great European War.

Becky watched as several pairs of mourning doves flitted around, their necks stretching with each step as they strolled the ground. Becky smiled to herself as she thought about how the doves stayed with the same partner for life. Cardinals did that, too. She rested her head against the tall back of the chair and would have liked to sit and daydream all afternoon. But an annoying version of "Corina, Corina" was being banged out on the family piano by the stout, cherubic, and sweaty Hugh Loomis. When he finally finished with an ivory-tickling flourish, his hands raised as high as his chin, everyone in the room clapped.

"Hugh, I had no idea you could play so divinely," Kitty Mackenzie said.

Hugh blushed at the compliment and looked to Becky to see if she shared in her mother's enthusiasm. Becky smiled and nodded politely.

"Why, thank you, Mrs. Mackenzie. I do like some of the new tunes I hear on the radio. But I must confess, my heart will forever be enslaved to the classics. Wagner especially."

Becky recoiled internally. She thought the only people who liked Wagner were undertakers and church organists. This was the latest man Kitty Mackenzie thought would make Becky a fine husband? Kitty had made a rather bold choice for Becky a while back who turned out to be a few cards short of a full deck and was now a permanent resident at Leavenworth Maximum Security Prison in Kansas.

"I know when I was in Paris that Grammy Louise insisted we attend the symphony at least once. I don't recall what they played the evening we were there. But I will say that only the finest of people do attend," Cousin Fanny offered.

She had been sitting in the lounge chair to Becky's left, also facing Hugh as he was seated behind the piano. In typical Fanny fashion, she was showing as much leg above the ankle as she could get away with and fluffed her blond curls every chance she got. Poor Hugh was having a devil of a time trying not to stare. Becky could hardly blame him, as he was no different from any other man who crossed Fanny's path. But Becky knew if she had to hear any more about Paris, she was going to lose her marbles.

"The symphony in Paris? That had to be wonderful," Hugh said, leering before he turned to Becky. "I've always thought Paris would make a wonderful honeymoon destination."

Becky began to cough as air went down the wrong pipe.

"Oh, Becky would be like a fish out of water in Paris," Fanny giggled. "I mean no disrespect, mind you. It's just that I know how finicky Parisians can be and, well, I do believe you'd be quite a sight in their eyes."

Becky did not miss Fanny's none-too-casual glance at the hem of her dress, which had gotten dirty during her morning excursion outside. She'd managed to hide it from her mother, but Becky should have known better than to expect Fanny not to study every inch of her armor for a chink prior to a male caller coming over.

"Hugh, would you care for another glass of lemonade? Or maybe some tea would suit you," Kitty interrupted like a referee stepping between two boxers when the bell rang.

"Thank you kindly, Mrs. Mackenzie. I think I'd like that very much." Hugh hoisted his pants over his slight paunch and smiled at Fanny, who stood from her lounging chair.

"I'll help you, Aunt Kitty," she said as she scooted dangerously close to Hugh in passing. Becky watched as Hugh chuckled then cleared his throat and watched Fanny exit the room before turning his attention to Becky as if he had suddenly remembered she was still there.

"It sure is a beautiful day, wouldn't you say, Miss Becky?" He withdrew a kerchief from his pocket and wiped his face.

"Yes. I had to cut my morning adventure short in order to greet you." Becky smiled sweetly on the outside but was writhing with boredom on the inside.

"Oh, I do apologize for that. What kind of adventure did you take?" He stepped closer, hooked the needlepointed ottoman with his foot, and pulled it close to Becky's chair.

"I just went to the Old Brick Cemetery. I find the company to be most entertaining. You'd be surprised at the words that come from a dead man's lips." She chuckled as she watched Hugh's response. At first his eyes bugged, but then they were swallowed by the wrinkles as he smiled.

"I heard you had a strange sense of humor, Rebecca Mackenzie." He pointed a finger at her as he leaned back. "I like that. I like a good bit about you."

"Really? May I ask who's been spinning yarns about little old me?" She looked out the window then back at Hugh, only to catch his eyes roaming over every part of her except her face.

"No one in particular," he said with a singsongy dip in his voice. "But I do get around town. I must confess, at first I wondered if you weren't a bad apple."

Becky laughed. "Me? A bad apple? Sounds like you've been talking to my cousin. I've never been to Paris, but I feel there are a number of good eggs around town that also haven't. If I'm in their company, I'll be happy as a clam."

"I wouldn't pay any attention to your cousin." Hugh leaned forward.

Becky could smell his aftershave lotion. It was flowery and sweet and rushed up her nose like a stampeding elephant to make her eyes slightly water.

"Too late," Becky chided.

"Oh, see. There's that sense of humor again." He wagged his finger as he chuckled. "No, I'm as serious as a heart attack, Miss Becky. Women like her in Paris might be fine to look at. But no one would consider her an honest woman."

Becky looked stone-faced at Hugh. Part of her wanted to clap the man on the back for saying what she had always thought. But there was a bigger part of her that took offence at his words.

"I believe you don't know much about me, Mr. Loomis. You know even less of my cousin. I'm not sure the men at the Elks Club would take too kindly to a gent who thinks he's the cat's pajamas parading around and giving his opinion of the women in their lives based on their looks." Just then, some movement caught her eye. "Daddy? Daddy, come in here. We've got company."

Becky stood up and waved excitedly to her father. She knew he wanted nothing more than to skate past the sitting room and avoid their visitor. Judge Mackenzie didn't care much for his wife's constant matchmaking attempts.

"Hello, sweetheart," he said before kissing Becky on the top of her head while at the same time sizing up Hugh Loomis. Judge stood a head taller than poor Hugh, and although Judge was at least thirty years his senior, he seemed to be in better shape than the young man.

"Daddy, this is Hugh Loomis. He was about to play another piece for us on the piano. Would you like to sit a spell and have a listen?" Becky was biting her tongue as she watched her father's expression. "He knows all the popular songs. I'm sure he'd be happy to play one for you. Wouldn't you, Hugh?"

"Hello, Mr. Mackenzie. I've heard a good bit about you, sir. It's a real pleasure..." Hugh stopped short as Judge put his hand up.

"No need for the formalities, son," Judge said. "I've got paperwork to tend to. But I'll be sure to mention to the fellas at the Elks Club that I made your acquaintance." He winked at his daughter and exited the room.

Becky folded her hands in front of her and looked at the distraught expression on Hugh's face with delight.

Just then Kitty and Fanny appeared with freshly filled crystal glasses of tea and small sandwiches on a silver platter.

"Now did I hear Becky say you were going to play another tune for us on the piano?" Kitty urged. "I think that would be absolutely delightful. What a wonderful idea, Rebecca."

"That's what he said." Becky took her seat again.

Hugh mustered up a sheepish smile and asked if there were any requests.

"Oh, I'd just love it if you'd play 'I'll Be With You in Apple Blossom Time,'" Fanny cooed. "I just adore that song."

Anyone would have thought Fanny had just asked Hugh to loosen his tie and take her for a spin in his jalopy the way he tittered and choked before cracking his knuckles and starting to play. Becky sat back in her chair and folded her arms. It was one thing for *her* to complain about Fanny. She knew exactly who and what she was. Becky knew if she were at some dump and the local talent was calling her cousin a floozy to the *n*th degree, she'd not bat an eye. But something didn't sit right with a gentleman caller under her roof insulting her most distasteful relative. It was wrong, and if anyone was going to call Fanny names in her house, it was going to be Becky. It certainly wasn't going to be the wet blanket tickling the ivories.

If she had to be honest, the piano man at the speakeasy she had gone to the previous night hadn't been much better. But the hooch she had been sipping while cutting the rug with some fella in a zoot suit had made the tunes sound swell.

As Hugh played, Fanny tried to belt out a few bars, snapping Becky out of her daydream. She was sure every cat in the neighborhood was going to come howling up the front porch steps at any minute. When she looked out the window, she saw something. It wasn't a cat. Instead, off in the distance, she saw a thin dark line in the blue sky. At first she thought it was a trick of the light. Or maybe it was a tree branch she was having trouble focusing on. But as she squinted, trying to see more clearly, the line became darker and thicker. It was smoke. Someone was burning something.

"Mama, isn't Old Man Ruthmeyer's farm off in that direction?" She pointed toward the window.

"Yes," Kitty said with her chin raised slightly. "Too close for my comfort. Why do you ask?"

"Has he ever burned anything on his property?" Becky looked at Hugh, who was still banging away on the piano. She cleared her throat loudly before he looked up and stopped just as Fanny was about to hit a high note.

"I do believe he burns trash every once in a while. When the heap gets too big for even him to tolerate, I suppose," Kitty added.

That possibility satisfied Becky as she watched the string of smoke curl and slither up into the air.

"Who is Mr. Ruthmeyer?" Hugh asked, wanting to stay part of the conversation. He looked at Kitty, but his eyes quickly snapped to Fanny's legs as she took her seat on the edge of the chaise again. Becky stared at him, cleared her throat, and gave him a smirk when he finally looked in her direction, realizing he'd been caught. His cheeks flashed red, and he tried to smile back but instead looked like he'd swallowed a fly.

"He's a neighbor on the far side of our property,"

Kitty replied. "I've only met the man once, but it was an introduction I could have done without."

"My goodness, Aunt Kitty. What happened?" Fanny asked.

"The man just had a lost look about him. He mumbled when he talked, and I could never see his teeth. To me, that meant he was hiding something." Kitty nodded and looked at her guest.

"Well, of course he was hiding something. It was probably Mrs. Tobin under his sheets," Becky chuckled.

"Rebecca Madeline Mackenzie, you bite your tongue," Kitty hissed.

"What?" Fanny was all ears, and Hugh seemed to perk up like a flower in a pot that had just gotten a sprinkling of rain.

"Mama, everyone knows the rumors." Becky shook her head.

"I don't. What rumors?" Fanny asked without hesitation.

"Becky, do not say another word." Kitty stood from her seat. "We do not entertain such gossip in our house."

"Some people think Mr. Ruthmeyer and Mrs. Tobin had a discreet affair that had been going on for several long years." Becky smiled at her mother.

"It's just a rumor. No one has ever seen them together or caught them doing anything. You know how rumors can start, right, Hugh? Someone says something about another person about the way they look or act, and the next thing you know, you've got the Whore of Babylon in your midst."

"Becky! Language, please!" Kitty began to fan herself. "Please excuse my daughter, Hugh. She loves to get a rile out of her mama."

"What does Mr. Ruthmeyer look like?" Fanny asked.

"Well, with a shave and a haircut, he might be a decent enough fellow. I think you should go calling on him, Fanny. He lives all by himself," Becky continued to tease as her mother became more embarrassed.

"I'll do no such thing." Fanny scooted in her seat and flipped her hair.

When Becky saw the look of distress on Kitty's face, she took a deep breath. "I'm sorry, Cousin Fanny. I was only teasing. Mama, I was just foolin'. Mr. Ruthmeyer keeps to himself, and I reckon he likes it that way."

"I couldn't imagine a life alone like that," Hugh said. "A house with a wife and lots of children. That's what makes a man." He puffed his chest and began to play random notes on the piano.

"I think that is a wonderful perspective, Hugh," Kitty gushed and looked approvingly at Becky.

Not wanting to cause her mother any further discomfort, Becky smiled back. Although she had no intention of ever entertaining Hugh Loomis again, Becky was willing to put on a good show for her mother's sake. But as she looked back out the window to the thin trail of smoke, she wondered about the man at the far end of their property.

John Ruthmeyer was a middle-aged farmer. If he'd nurtured his land the way he nurtured the chip on his shoulder, he would have been the most successful farmer in Savannah, Georgia. But as it was, he found himself too busy in a constant war with anyone and everyone within a fifty-mile radius of his homestead. Everyone except Judge Mackenzie. There seemed to be some gentleman's agreement between the two that kept John Ruthmeyer on one side of the fence and Judge on the other.

Becky had come across Mr. Ruthmeyer on a couple of occasions when she was out at the cemetery. He drank a good bit and seemed to forever be looking for something. His expression was sour, with squinting, beady eyes, and his jaw was perpetually clenched. Thankfully, he never noticed Becky when he was out prowling around the tombstones. Whatever he had lost out there kept him distracted, his eyes scouring the ground and his hands deep in his pockets. Without letting her wild imagination take a rest, Becky always guessed he was looking for a jar of pennies he'd buried when he was drunk and had since forgotten. Or maybe it was moonshine he stole from the people who lived on the swamps. Those moonshiners were not to be messed with when it came to their product. There wasn't a gun-carrying gangster in the city tougher than those boys in their worn-out overalls and bare feet.

Becky listened to Hugh and Fanny make more noise than music and imagined the trouble Mr. Ruthmeyer would be in if he had indeed stolen their moonshine. It would have been exciting and stupid all at the same time. But as she watched the smoke, expecting it to continue rising in a gray, feathery plume, she started to see a change. It wasn't going out. The clouds were getting bigger and darker. It was then that Becky didn't think the fire was at Mr. Ruthmeyer's place but that part of the tobacco field had to be on fire.

She jumped up from her seat, making Hugh hit the wrong notes and Fanny choke on her words.

"I think there's more than a trash fire, Mama." Becky walked to the window. "Doesn't that look like something bigger is burning? Like it might be our tobacco."

Kitty got up from her seat and stood next to her daughter. She looked in the direction Becky was pointing and gasped. "Judge! Judge!"

Judge's heavy boots could be heard clomping down the hardwood floor from the kitchen. Within seconds, he appeared in the sitting room.

"What's the matter?"

"There's a fire! Looks like our property. Judge, what do we do?" Kitty asked while wringing her hands.

In two long strides, Judge was at the window and looking in the direction of the smoke.

"Hugh Loomis? Is your automobile out front?" His voice was loud and firm.

"Yes, sir," he stuttered.

"Then what are you waiting for? Let's go." Judge stomped past Becky, Kitty, and Fanny toward the front door with Hugh clumsily hurrying behind him.

Becky wasn't going to wait for an invitation. She hurried on tiptoe behind the two men sneaking out just as the screen door was about to bang shut.

Before they could say a word, she was in the rumble seat of Hugh's car, ready to go.

"Now, Becky, I don't think this is any place for a lady," Hugh started.

"Son, don't even bother trying to tell her no," Judge said without looking at his daughter. "Let's step on it." He pointed in the direction of the old dirt road that would run right in front of the Ruthmeyer farm. Within seconds, all that was left in front of the Mackenzie house was a plume of dust and the wheel tracks in the dry red earth. The smell of smoke was in the air, and the sky over the far acres of Mackenzie property was getting darker by the minute.

I've never seen a fire outside of the fireplace, Becky thought. *I do hope it isn't too bad. Daddy will be in a state if it spreads across the fields.*

"Step on it, boy! This is a fire, not a dance we're going to," Judge ordered.

Becky saw that Hugh was distressed at having to speed his jalopy down a dirt road with debris and mud coating the sides. She immediately thought a man like Hugh would be more concerned about his vehicle than a man's crops. It was a fact she'd be sure to share with her mother upon their return.

"There's the fence!" Judge shouted. "Turn here and follow along."

It was the barbed wire fence that separated the Mackenzie property line from Mr. Ruthmeyer's. Becky squinted down the row to see where the fire was. From her point of view, she saw nothing. No flames. No smoke. Then it came into view. It wasn't the field that was on fire. It was a house. Mr. Ruthmeyer's house. And as they got closer, Becky was sure she could hear screaming.

CHAPTER TWO

The Ruthmeyer homestead was a simple place. It could have been nice with a new coat of paint or maybe a garden of sunflowers growing alongside of it. But as it was, John Ruthmeyer didn't see the need for such upkeep.

Now the chipped and faded paint along the sides of the house was all that contained the blazing fire inside. Each window on the first floor glowed with monstrous flames. Black soot clung to the windowsills as smoke poured out. Somewhere, someone else had seen the smoke, and the clanging bell of a couple of fire trucks could be heard in the distance. They'd never arrive in time to save anything.

"Stay here, Becky," Judge said to his daughter as he got out of the car.

Hugh followed for no other reason than he thought he should.

Becky did as her father asked and remained in the rumble seat. The smell of smoke would cling to her dress and hair for days. But it was the sound above it all, above the crackling fire and the collapsing of beams inside, that would stay with Becky. It was almost inhuman.

"Daddy, there's someone inside!" she yelled.

"What?" Judge stopped for a moment.

"Don't you hear it? The screaming. Don't you hear it coming from inside the house? Daddy, I think Mr. Ruthmeyer is still inside."

Judge held still for a moment and listened.

"I think that's just the wind. Maybe a gust catching through some glass." Hugh shook his head. "This is too much for you, Becky. You don't belong at a scene like this."

Judge paid no mind to Hugh and looked sternly at his daughter. Although no one in the Mackenzie household spoke about it openly, Judge knew his daughter was different and had special talents that couldn't be explained.

Becky, also paying no mind to Hugh, climbed out

of the rumble seat and clutched her father's strong arm. "Up there! In that room!"

Judge whirled around and ran toward the burning building. Standing just feet from the inferno, he shouted over and over at the small window at the very tip-top of the house. The flames inside had not reached that high yet. If there was anyone inside, there was a chance, a small sliver, that they might be able to wriggle out of the window and suffer a few broken bones instead of death.

"John! John, are you up there?" Judge shouted, his face already black and drenched in sweat.

Hugh stood nearby in case Judge called to him. He looked lost and confused.

"She took my legs!" was all Judge could hear John screaming. "Give me back my legs! Give me back my legs!"

"John! Get to the window! The firemen are here, and they can catch you!" Judge ordered but to no avail. Mr. Ruthmeyer had gone insane with terror.

Becky stood by and heard his cries. No matter what the rumors were about the man or how he lived his life, this wasn't anything she'd wish on even her worst enemy. To die alone in flames, Becky thought, should be the cleansing process that sent a person straight into Jesus's arms. Any sins were paid in full.

Just as the fire trucks pulled up, Judge was screaming at the top of his lungs for Mr. Ruthmeyer to get to the window. Everyone saw a hand go past the pane. He was trying. He was feeling his way around. It had to be black as pitch inside that small attic room, with no air to breathe. Becky had no idea she was holding her breath, but just as Mr. Ruthmeyer was able to get the window open, the entire inside of the building collapsed. The roof caved in as flames writhed and snaked their way over the shingles, consuming everything. Sparks and smoke blew toward the tobacco plants. The firefighters did what they could to prevent the fire from spreading, but there was little else they could do.

It was when the Judge and Hugh joined the firefighters, telling them that they believed Mr. Ruthmeyer was still inside, that Becky saw the woman emerge from the nearby line of trees. She was wild-eyed and crying. Some of her hair had fallen from the bun in the back of her head and clung in dark wisps to her sweaty cheeks.

"John!" she screamed. "John! John! Oh no, John! No! No! No!"

It was Mrs. Tobin. Becky's heart broke for her.

She might have been in an adulterous relationship, but the pain on her face at this very moment made her appear to age right before Becky's eyes. Mr. Ruthmeyer had been consumed by the fire just as something in this poor woman was consumed as well.

Before she even thought to go to Mrs. Tobin and comfort her, the woman ran toward the building. It took two firefighters to hold her back. She was willing to end her own life in those flames too. Was she so much in love?

Becky thought of the man she loved and considered if she'd do the same. Just as she was about to reveal the answer to herself, she saw someone else emerge from the trees. Nothing about her looked familiar to Becky. She wore a white linen dress with a purple printed scarf wrapped around her head. Her skin was dark like coffee and hung off her bones in crinkled flaps. Plus her body looked frail and thin beneath the loose-fitting clothes. She stood at the edge of the trees and didn't move but watched what was happening with morbid fascination.

In the meantime, several cars that Becky recognized pulled up to help. Teddy Rockdale, Becky's dear friend and neighbor since childhood, arrived with his father and what looked like a couple of his cousins. There were also some of the other folk who had farms out this way.

The ladies and young 'uns just watched as the men all pitched in. There were quite a few lollygaggers among the bunch who didn't help, and many were more interested in taking notice of Mrs. Tobin, who was on her knees sobbing into her hands.

Becky couldn't take it. Adulterer or no, no woman should ever be left so alone in her pain. After squaring her shoulders, Becky proceeded to hurry over to Mrs. Tobin. But before she could reach her, the small black woman with the scarf around her head shouted something Becky didn't quite make out. But something told her to stop in her place, thinking the woman was addressing her. Their eyes met, and Becky saw just sharp, black discs staring at her.

Before Becky could inquire what the strange woman wanted, Mrs. Tobin got up from her knees, turned around, and went to the lady. Becky's first thoughts were that maybe the woman was her nurse or caretaker. The Tobins had no children. After losing each attempt, they had given up. But if Mrs. Tobin found comfort in keeping a nurse around, Becky certainly wasn't going to find any fault with it.

The women disappeared into the trees and were not seen again.

Judge's clothes were black and torn in places. For all his bad manners and clumsy conversation, Hugh was not much better off than Judge, as he had also rolled up his sleeves when the time came. It took three-quarters of an hour for the fire to finally go out, leaving behind nothing but smoldering ashes, blackened wooden beams, and one gruesome element: the charred body of John Ruthmeyer.

"I just don't understand it," Becky heard one of the firemen say to Judge. "It was like the water was evaporating before it hit the fire. I've never seen such a thing. Not in all my years. "

"You did your best. The house was already gone when you got here," Judge soothed as he put his hand on the man's shoulder. "Any idea what could have started it? It's been quite dry these past couple weeks. Maybe a stray cinder from the fireplace or a cigarette."

"That might be, Mr. Mackenzie. I couldn't rightly say. Mr. Ruthmeyer didn't smoke as far as I know. I thought I picked up the smell of gasoline. Right now, I can't be sure. But we should have been able to salvage something. It was like we tried to put the flames out with steam. I don't know what could have made the heat so high." The fireman reached under his hat and scratched his head. "I just never saw anything like that. Not in all my years."

Becky returned to the car and waited for her father and Hugh. She turned her back as the men ventured into the glowing ashes to retrieve Mr. Ruthmeyer's body. When the gory task was complete and the body had been placed away from the smoldering structure and covered, Judge and Hugh returned to the car. It was bad enough the two men smelled of smoke, but only a person with no nose would escape the faint odor of burnt flesh that was clinging to them.

The people who had come to stare still meandered around, trying to get a closer glimpse of the destruction of the property and its owner. If everyone thought that fire had spread fast, wait until the news of this tragedy and the appearance of Mrs. Tobin hit the streets.

Unlike the regular folks wanting to hear the gossip, Becky felt herself most disturbed by the woman in the purple head scarf.

"Daddy, who was that woman who tended to Mrs. Tobin?" Becky asked.

"I didn't see any lady," Judge replied and then let out a deep sigh.

"You didn't see that woman lead her back through the tree line?" Becky asked further. "I've never seen her before, and we know just about everyone in Savannah and the surrounding counties."

"What are you getting at, Becky?" Judge snapped.

"Nothing, Daddy. I'm sorry." She saw sadness in her father's eyes. He hadn't been able to help save Mr. Ruthmeyer or any of his property. That sort of disappointment always weighed heavily on a man of solid character.

The rest of the ride back home was quiet. Once they pulled up and Kitty stepped out on the porch, she nearly screamed at the sight of her husband. She fussed over Judge and Hugh, who she instructed to go around to the back of the house, where Moxley, the family butler, would get them water and soap to clean up with.

"And you. Oh, my poor dear," she said to Becky, who up until this point hadn't paid any attention to her own appearance. "Come and take that dress off in the foyer. Fanny, get your cousin her robe, and tell Lucretia to run a bath."

Becky looked down and saw she was also covered in black soot. She didn't think the smoke had come close to her, but her clothes and hands

26

said differently. The natural folds in her skin were caked in black, and she was sure she smelled horrible. But that was of little consequence. Who was that woman, and why had Mrs. Tobin followed her away from the house? Becky had a gut feeling she had something to do with this tragedy.

CHAPTER THREE

s usual, once the sun set on the Mackenzie plantation, Teddy Rockdale appeared in his new jalopy wearing spiffy duds and ready to take Becky to any speakeasy they could agree on. Of course, Fanny would also be joining them, and since Hugh Loomis had been invited to clean up and stay for supper, he was crammed into the rumble seat.

"I could have fit all of us in my boiler," he offered.

"Hey, that's a mighty nice gesture, Hugh, ol' boy, but this way, we can all get to know each other better. And get used to the close quarters, because we'll be picking up one more." Teddy lifted his chin.

"We are?" Fanny batted her eyes.

"We can't go dancing without Martha," Becky said as she smoothed out the front of her dress. She was wearing a gold getup with long strings of black beads across the front. "Do I still smell of smoke?"

"I don't know," Teddy replied. "If you do, I probably do, too. What a sight. I knew it was only a matter of time before something happened to that fellow."

"What do you mean?" Becky asked.

"Mr. Ruthmeyer was as mean as a snake. I'd bet that by now, half the town is lit after celebrating his demise," he replied.

"That's horrible." Becky wrinkled her nose. "I don't know much about the man, but he was alive in that fire. If those same people were to have heard him crying out, they might not be so uppity."

"So where are we going?" Fanny asked.

"Let's let Martha pick," Teddy suggested.

Becky smirked, since she had known for some time that Teddy and Martha were sweet on each other.

Fanny wasn't used to coming in second place, and it was obvious her nose was out of joint. "I do hope she knows of a nice place. When I was in Paris, even the most simple bistros were more elegant than the finest clubs here in the States. They just tend to handle themselves better than we do here," Fanny babbled.

"Hit the gas, Teddy. I'm itching for some excitement," Becky said.

Once they pulled up in front of Martha Bourdeaux's house, it was seconds before the girl was dashing out the door and hopping into the back seat.

"Hi, Fanny. Who's the new fella?" Martha asked, jerking her thumb over her shoulder after giving Teddy and Becky a peck on the cheek.

"Martha, I'd like you to meet Hugh Loomis. My mother invited him over for tea today, and he's decided to move in." Becky rolled her eyes.

"Well, hello, Mr. Loomis." Martha offered her hand. "Have you all heard about the commotion today? Of course you have. John Ruthmeyer lived a stone's throw from your property. Becky, tell me none of your father's crops were harmed."

"No. Not a leaf."

"Well, thank God for that. In my humble opinion, that is cause to celebrate. Where are we going?" Martha pulled a cigarette from her purse and lit it.

"Teddy said we were leaving it to you. Fanny asked that we go somewhere refined, you know, like they have in Paris," Becky replied.

"Oh, I believe I know just the place. The Crazy Calico. I think the word used to describe it is rustic.

Is it just me, or do any of you smell smoke? And I don't mean from my ciggy," Martha asked.

Hugh apologized and proceeded to tell Martha how he and Judge had arrived at the fire. Teddy pitched in his two cents, and before anyone realized it, they were all talking at the same time.

"It was horrible," Becky said.

"Was Mr. Ruthmeyer really inside?" Martha asked.

"The firemen retrieved him once the fire was out," Hugh added.

"Did Mrs. Tobin really make such a scene?" Fanny gasped.

"I didn't see her. But the way the smoke was blowing, I didn't see much of anything," Teddy replied.

The conversation went on like this until Teddy pulled the car down a quiet street with rows of simple, cheap houses.

"All right. Everybody out," Martha said as she stood in the back seat and swung her legs out the window and slid to her feet. She linked her arm with Becky's.

Hugh joined Teddy with a quick question about his automobile. Fanny pushed her way between them.

"Would you boys mind if I walked with you? I feel that drive has left me breathless and fear I may lose my legs if I'm not careful."

"Of course, Fanny," Teddy said without giving her a second look. He had grown used to her like someone might grow used to a needy cat. Give it a tickle under the chin, and it'll be content.

Hugh, on the other hand, was struck stupid when she pulled him toward her, making sure to accidentally brush her bosom against his arm. They followed Becky and Martha down the sidewalk until they reached the alley.

"Where are we going?" Fanny asked.

"The Crazy Calico," Teddy whispered.

"It looks rather...dangerous," Fanny said, snapping Hugh out of his stupor. He looked around nervously.

"Don't worry, Becky knows people." Teddy smiled like a crocodile.

"Becky? What kind of a lady *knows people*?" Hugh asked, his hopes of winning Becky's hand suddenly doused with cold water.

"Oh, you'll see, Hugh ol' boy."

They all gathered around a dirty door that could have easily been overlooked. There was no light over it and no signs or even an arrow painted on the dirty brick wall to indicate there was a club there. But as Becky knocked, a small square in the middle of the door opened.

"Who's that?" Becky stood on tiptoes, her fingers on the sill of the small window. "Is that Patsy or Bluto?"

"Who's askin'?" the grumbly voice behind the door asked.

"Now, Patsy, I haven't been gone for that long, have I? You can't forget your favorite gal, can you?" Becky flirted.

"Becky? I almost didn't recognize you. You changed your hair," Patsy replied before shutting the little window and opening the door. "In this light, I can't see the red. You know how much I love redheads. That fiery temper."

"Patsy, you're so full of hot air. Let us in before we're picked up for loitering," Becky said as she slipped inside.

Patsy was a strong fellow who wore a button-down shirt open at the collar without a tie and had his sleeves rolled up. His trousers were high up his waist and frayed around the cuffs.

"I gotta tell you, Beck, you might want to find another dive to go to tonight," Patsy said, stooping a little so Becky could hear him.

"Why? What's stirring?"

"You heard about that fire today?" Patsy said, looking into the main room of revelers then back at her.

"Sure," she replied without going into any greater detail.

"Well, there are a couple of fellows who have in no uncertain terms made it clear they are quite happy with the outcome of that fire," Patsy said. "They got my neck hairs up. There will be a brawl before the night is over. You can take that to the bank. On any other night, I'd pull up a chair for you. But I don't think you should stay tonight. Not tonight."

"Patsy, we came all this way. Don't send us away dry," Becky pouted.

Patsy took a deep breath and looked over his shoulder then back at Becky. "Promise you won't stay too long?"

"Cross my heart," Becky flirted then took hold of Martha's hand and sauntered in. Martha blew a kiss to Patsy. Teddy shook his hand and introduced Fanny and Hugh.

The Crazy Calico held a maximum of twenty people, but at least twice that many were crammed inside. The long bar that took up the north wall was completely full with fellows in their work blues and bibs. Sprinkled between them were ladies in their frocks and stockings rolled to their knees who patted their finger waves as they sized up Becky and her group. Still, even with almost every inch of space taken, Becky managed to find a small table that she and her friends could gather around.

The place was very dark due to the years of smoke and dirt that had accumulated on the walls. The lights were nothing more than a couple of bulbs hanging from the ceiling and a couple of storm lamps behind the bar. The floor was covered with peanut shells and sawdust.

"We are like fish out of water here," Fanny whispered.

"Relax," Martha said as she leaned against Becky. "The gin is just as wet here as anywhere else."

"You said a mouthful," Teddy said. "Hugh, ol' boy, come with me. These ladies aren't going to water themselves." Teddy clapped Hugh on the back, making him cough.

As the men strolled up to the bar, Becky looked around and saw a couple of rather grim fellows looking in her direction.

"What's wrong with those guys?" Martha whispered in Becky's ear.

"Don't worry about it. They're probably just lit," Becky said. Although she was sure she'd seen those men somewhere before. They'd never be allowed in Willie's club dressed the way they were. And they weren't from the juke joint on the edge of the creek. As she flipped through the list of speakeasies she knew, nothing rang a bell.

"They are making me rather uneasy," Fanny said as she adjusted her skirt high on her knees and leaned back in her chair. If this was how she acted when she was uneasy, Becky was sure her dress would fall off completely if she were relaxed.

When Teddy and Hugh returned with drinks, Martha was the first to notice that Hugh had something different in his hand.

"That doesn't look like a champagne cocktail." Becky pointed to the Mason jar he was holding.

"Moonshine," he said proudly.

"You ever drink moonshine, Hugh? I don't know if that is such a good idea," Martha said. "Teddy could pour it in the gas tank, and we'd be able to drive for miles."

"When in Rome," Hugh said and raised his jar.

The rest of them took their drinks, raised them high, and clanked them together as they toasted to the Crazy Calico.

It didn't take long for the regulars to forget about Becky and her friends. Soon the piano was playing loudly, and people were dancing in the tiny square of space in the middle of the room, shouting to one another and laughing.

One of the fellows who had been staring at Becky strolled up to the table. "Care to dance?" he asked.

"I'd love to," she said without hesitation. "Martha, make sure my ice doesn't melt."

Within seconds, they were crammed onto the tiny dance floor with the other partiers. The man held her tightly around the waist and was a surprisingly good dancer. He swung her around in that small space as if she weighed no more than a feather.

"You're not from around here," he said in her ear.

"You're daft. I'm born and raised in Savannah. Ain't no part of this city I don't know." She smiled sweetly. "In fact, I heard all about that fire this morning. I'll bet I knew all about it before anyone."

The man's steps slowed, and he tightened his grip around her waist.

"Hey, now." She pushed against his chest. "Don't act like some palooka. Turn me loose, or I'll…"

"You'll what?" he said in her ear. "You shouldn't be shooting your mouth off about that fire. You don't know anything about it."

"You're wrong. I was there," she said with the most angelic smile. "I heard him screaming, and I don't believe that fire started itself."

She stared into the man's beady eyes as he squinted nervously at her.

"I'm going to tell you something, girlie-girl. Ruthmeyer got what was coming to him. Everyone knew it was only a matter of time before he got his comeuppance."

"Comeuppance for what?" Becky pushed.

The man sneered at her and shook his head. He licked his lips then swallowed as if he was getting ready to tell her a long tale. But he didn't say anything and instead stared at her.

"What's the matter? Cat got your tongue?" Becky continued. "You don't have to tell me anything. But I have a way of knowing things without people saying a word."

"I wouldn't go saying that too loudly around some people, girlie-girl," the man said. "And I certainly wouldn't tell anyone I had any contact with anyone by the name of Ruthmeyer unless you want to suffer the same fate."

He looked down at her, his feet no longer moving to the rhythm of the music and his grip around her waist even tighter than before.

Just then, Becky noticed a strange symbol scratched into the wall. Had she not looked directly at it, she would have dismissed it as wear and tear or maybe graffiti scratched by some drunken patron. It was a circle the size of a human head with a slash through it.

"What is that symbol scratched in the wall?"

Becky had hoped her dance partner would turn to look, but instead he clenched his teeth. He pulled her even closer to him. She could feel his hot breath against her cheek. Becky Mackenzie had dealt with her share of grabby gents who threw back one too many, but this man didn't smell of alcohol. He was sober, and that made Becky very scared.

"You're hurting me," she said between tight lips.

"Oh, you don't know what I'm capable of. We aren't scared of people like you here," the man said, a sinister smile stretching across his lips.

"People like me?" Becky's face twisted in a mixture of discomfort and confusion.

"Hey, hey, hey." Hugh suddenly appeared, his nose red and his eyes glazed over. "Good sir, do you mind if I cut in?"

"I most certainly do." The man scowled.

"My dogs are barking. I think a sip of something cold would do me some good." Becky tried to pull away, but this strange, angry dance partner was not ready to let her go.

"Now, friend, I think I'd like to dance with this lady." Hugh poked the man sternly on the shoulder. Hugh was soft all over, and perhaps if he were sober, he would have decided against cutting in. But as it was, that moonshine he was sipping gave him courage he probably didn't know he had.

"I ain't your friend," the man said.

"Come on. We're all friends here," Becky insisted, finally pulling out of her dance partner's grip and slipping her arm through Hugh's. "We can have another dance later."

"I don't think so," the man replied.

By now everyone was watching. The regulars at the bar had turned around in their seats to get a better view. The ladies were shaking their heads, whispering to each other as they looked disgusted with Becky and her entourage. The music had also stopped, and even the bartender, a huge, hairy man with an apron around his waist, looked like he wanted to box their ears.

"I think you owe the lady an apology," Hugh said. "You might not be used to dealing with a woman of her caliber, but I assure you that your actions are those of a backwoods rogue." It seemed the moonshine made him not only brave but poetic.

"What did you just say?" the man asked, causing half the patrons in the joint to stand up, showing their solidarity with him.

"He didn't say anything. It was the moonshine that did the talking. You can't blame a man for what he says after drinking that stuff," Becky said, frantically waving to Martha, Teddy, and Fanny. "But we've obviously caused quite a stir. We don't want trouble, so we'll be on our way."

"I don't think any of you are going anywhere," Becky's dance partner hissed. "You ask a lot of questions. People around here don't like strangers snooping around."

"What questions? I just mentioned knowing about the fire at the Ruthmeyer place," Becky stuttered as she inched toward the door. It was as if all the air had been sucked out of the place.

"Benny. Lock that back door."

Becky looked at the man who had up until a few minutes ago been simply dancing with her and thought perhaps it was all a ruse. People in places like this sometimes picked out the rubes or the greenhorns in order to roll them for their money. But Becky and her friends weren't rubes.

"Patsy!" Becky shouted.

Within seconds, the bouncer was at her side. His hands clenched and unclenched as his bulging eyes scanned the room. From where Becky was standing, it looked like Patsy was hoping for a brawl. He had that look of a man who'd been cooped up for too long, and stretching his legs just wasn't going to cut it. Only a fight would put out the flame.

"I think you are right, Patsy. We'll be leaving," Becky said.

After grabbing Hugh with one hand and Martha with the other, she let Patsy lead them safely to the door. Teddy tended to Fanny, who was clinging tightly to him.

"Didn't I tell you?" Patsy said as he pushed them out the door. "Didn't I say it was off its rocker in there?"

"You did," Becky said with her chin to her chest and a pout on her lips.

"Come back when it isn't so hot outside. You won't run into that group when it starts to get cold outside," he added.

"Okay. Why is that?" Becky scratched her head.

"I guess they just don't like the cold." Patsy shrugged.

"Let me tell you something, friend." Hugh

looked up about six inches to see into Patsy's face. "I don't care who you are or what you do. I will not let you continue on your way without some advice."

"Here it comes." Patsy rolled his eyes.

"If you don't grab what you want…there will be too much…and everything in between. Don't forget it." Hugh patted Patsy's shoulder, turned on his heel, and with the precision of a bumblebee, started to walk in the direction of the car.

"I don't know about you guys, but I think we ought to scram, and fast," Martha said while looking over her shoulder as the group walked down the alley.

"What did you say to that man?" Fanny asked. "I swear I saw his face turn half a dozen shades of red."

"I was just asking about the fire. They all seemed to know about it and Mr. Ruthmeyer. I was just making conversation," Becky replied innocently.

"I don't know. I think we ought to take Hugh back to Becky's place. He isn't going to last much longer." Teddy pointed to Hugh, who was standing at the opening of the alley, swaying as if a tropical breeze was gently blowing.

"I agree. Tonight's a bust," Becky added.

Everyone helped Hugh along and quickly got him

to Teddy's jalopy, where he promptly fell into a deep sleep, complete with snoring and flatulating.

"Poor Hugh." Martha shook her head. "I don't know what would possess any man to drink moonshine. My daddy said he's known more than one man to go blind from the stuff."

"Stick to gin, champagne, and rye in the bathtub like civilized bootleggers," Teddy pretended to complain and made Martha laugh.

Becky smiled, but she was distracted by what she'd learned from that man in the speakeasy. She didn't think she'd be visiting the Crazy Calico again any time soon. But she couldn't forget how he had looked when she mentioned the fire or that strange symbol carved on the wall.

CHAPTER FOUR

"*I* hope you're happy with yourself," Fanny whispered to Becky when she came down the stairs the following morning.

Becky wrinkled her face, pinched her eyebrows together, and pulled her wild red hair away from her face. Even though she'd barely had anything to drink the prior night, her head was foggy and ached at the temples.

"What?"

"Hugh Loomis never made it home last night. In fact, he never made it out of the driveway. Your father's employees from the field found him slumped over, sound asleep, still in the driveway."

Becky chuckled.

"It isn't funny. Do you realize the rumors that are

going to circulate?" Fanny straightened her back. "Why, it'll bring shame on the entire house."

"Hugh Loomis took three sips of moonshine and got knocked on his keister? That's the headline for today's news? I think the Mackenzie household will survive the scandal," Becky said as she elbowed her way past Fanny to the bathroom.

It didn't take long for Kitty to find her.

"Out, right now, young lady," Kitty ordered.

Becky came out of the bathroom, her face freshly washed and her hair pinned back. She looked fresh as a daisy, a fact that rather surprised her mother.

"Now, Mama, before you get wound up, it was Hugh's decision to get himself some moonshine. We all advised against it. But you know how it is trying to tell a man what to do. Especially at a speakeasy." Becky batted her lashes.

"Do you know your father's foreman and several of the field hands saw him this morning?" Kitty asked, folding her arms in front of her.

"He said he was fine to drive himself home. He insisted," Becky replied.

"This is shameful. Do you know his mother was up pacing the floor all night? What is she going to say about us after this?" Kitty tapped her foot and tilted her head, glaring at Becky.

"Well, she better not say a darn thing. It was her son who drank moonshine. No one held him down with a funnel in his mouth." Becky folded her arms and tilted her head, mimicking her mother.

Kitty took a deep breath and let her arms fall to her sides. "I just don't know what I'm going to do with you. I think you owe Hugh an apology."

"What? What for?"

"For not taking better care," Kitty replied.

"Well, I didn't know he was as helpless as a newborn kitten. I sure will, Mama. I'll pen him the longest, most sincere apology I can write."

"You won't have to write it. He's downstairs with your father." With that, Kitty turned and walked into the master bedroom, shutting the door behind her.

Becky stood in the hallway with her mouth hanging open. It had to be past eight o'clock. How could Hugh still be loitering around?

After swallowing hard, patting her hair into place, and pulling her robe shut tightly around her, Becky marched downstairs. Moxley came from her father's den and gave Becky a nod while putting his finger to his lips. She waved and nodded back.

Through the door to the den, Becky heard her father speaking softly but firmly to an audience that didn't make a peep.

"It's not the way to win a woman over, son. Especially not one like my daughter," Judge said. "And I know that you won't be spinning tales about things that didn't happen. Sometimes opportunities arise for a man to do some bragging, embellishing, fibbing, and the attention of one's constituents blinds him to the severity of his actions. We aren't going to have any situations like that, now, are we?"

Becky didn't hear a sound, but her father's reply made it clear that his audience was in total agreement with him.

"I knew you were a man of honor, son. And I welcome you back in my house at any time."

Becky rolled her eyes at her father's last comment. What in the world would Hugh Loomis ever want to come back here for? His mama certainly wouldn't want him coming back. With that final thought, Becky cleared her throat and entered the room. A fit of laughter raced up her throat but got choked back as she straightened her posture and smiled at Judge.

"Good morning, Daddy."

"Good morning, Becky," Judge said with a wink.

"Good morning, Hugh. Why, I didn't expect you to come back and see me so soon," she said, adjusting her robe and patting her hair back. It was so painfully obvious that Hugh had the hangover to end all hangovers that Becky wasn't sure she'd be able to keep a straight face.

He was sweating terribly. After sleeping in his car, his clothes were wrinkled and dirty from the dew collecting on him in the early hours and the dust kicking up with just the slightest breeze then clinging to the moisture. But his eyes said it all. They were the most bloodshot red Becky had ever seen, peeking from black baggy caverns.

"I never made it home. I passed out in my car," he replied bashfully as Judge clapped him on the shoulder before leaving them alone. Becky could tell the gesture rattled his brain, making him wince.

"Well, I told you that moonshine wasn't a good idea," she soothed.

"I should have listened." He rubbed his hand over his head and winced again. Becky had been there a few times. Although she'd never in a million years drink moonshine, she'd tossed back a few too many martinis on occasion and paid the price the following day.

"Have you had any coffee? I can have Lucretia scramble you up some eggs." Becky truly felt bad for the gent.

"You have the natural instincts to make a swell

wife. I'd never say a bad word about you. You've been nothing but kind and considerate of me and…" he gushed.

Becky smiled. She was sure he was still drunk, but even if he wasn't, those were not the words she wanted to hear.

"Becky, I believe that if you'll give me a chance, I will do everything within my power to make you happy and…"

Before another word was spoken, Fanny sashayed into the room. "Oh, I'm sorry. I didn't know you were receiving guests at this hour, and still in your nightclothes." Fanny snickered. She extended her hand to Hugh, who sucked in his gut and got immediately to his feet.

"What was it you were saying?" Becky asked, watching Hugh's nervous, bloodshot eyes flit from her to Fanny's cleavage and back again.

"Oh, well, I really must be going." Hugh cleared his throat.

"Yes, Mother is waiting," Becky snapped, glad to be rid of him. She turned and left the room, heading to the kitchen, where her little friend Teeter was sitting at the table and writing in a book.

"Mornin', Miss Becky," Lucretia said as she stood

at the stove, stirring some grits while tending to crackling bacon.

"Good morning, Lucretia. Morning, Teeter. What are you writing there?"

"I'm practicing my letters." He held up the clunky, scribbly ABC's he was working on.

"Well, that is mighty fine. When you get to Z, will you write me a letter?" Becky asked.

"I sure will. And I'll write one to Mama and Pa and Miss Kitty and Mister Judge and Pastor Reed and…"

"You're going to be awful busy." Becky winked.

She poured herself a cup of coffee then headed back to her room. As soon as she shut the door, she took a seat at her vanity and watched out the window as Hugh Loomis climbed into his boiler and drove off. She hoped the grinding sound of the gears rattled his teeth and made his head pound. It wasn't that he was such a bad person. But he shouldn't have insinuated marriage to one woman while his lust for another was on full display.

She took a sip of coffee, retrieved her sketch-book, and began to doodle. Before long, she had drawn out the face of the man she had danced with the night before. She also scribbled the circle with the line through it. It bothered her that this symbol was scratched into the wall at the Crazy Calico. Part of her wanted to go back. If she could find Patsy, he might know what it was all about.

But it would have to wait. After the previous night being cut short, Martha and Teddy were ready to make up for lost time. Teddy moseyed over around one in the afternoon to tell Becky to put on her finest duds and bring bail money. She was thrilled.

CHAPTER FIVE

illie's Club was surrounded by trees and off the beaten path, but when Teddy pulled up to the joint, there were cars parked as far as they could see.

"What are they doing, giving booze away?" Teddy asked.

"I hope so," Martha replied. "Find a spot, Jeeves."

"Of course, Madame." Teddy spun the car into the first spot he could find, and within seconds, the entire group—including Fanny—was inside with their hands holding drinks and their toes tapping.

"I have to admit, cousin, this is a much more respectable establishment than the Crazy Calico," Fanny said as she sipped her champagne.

"Yes, Becky. Why would you want to go to a

dirty, illegal speakeasy with shady characters when you could go to a moderately cleaner illegal speakeasy with shady characters?" Martha asked before tossing back her second drink in fifteen minutes.

"Me? You're the one who picked that joint." Becky shook her head. She was ready to continue arguing in her own defense, but an all-too-familiar face had just walked in.

"Well, Teddy, Fanny, it looks like our time with Miss Becky is over. She's more interested in that cool sip of water that just walked in," Martha teased.

"I haven't talked to Adam in ages," Becky said while swinging one leg across the other.

"Oh, have you two had a falling out?" Fanny asked quickly while batting her eyes and straightening her posture. She had the attention of just about every gent in the place, but that wasn't enough. Now that Adam White had walked in, it was a completely different ball game.

"None of your business," Becky snapped as she watched Adam, who was scanning the room. As soon as their eyes met, she looked away.

"Now, don't get fitsy with your cousin, Beck." Martha patted Becky's hand. "I'm sure she's just looking out for you. Ain't I right, Fanny?"

"Of course," Fanny said as she looked at Adam as if he were a slab of raw beef and she was a wolf.

Adam White *was* a tall glass of cool water. He elbowed his way to the bar, nodded to the fellows on either side, and then turned to focus on Becky.

"Aren't you going to go talk to him?" Martha whispered in Becky's ear.

"No."

"Why not? You can't still be sore about what he did." Martha kept her voice low. "He's from good stock, even if he is a Northerner. He was raised to be a gentleman. And the burden of being a gentleman means you act that way no matter what cat might be rubbing on your leg."

"I know, Martha." Becky shook her head.

Not long ago, there had been an incident. It wasn't long after Fanny had come to town to stay indefinitely with the Mackenzies. Becky had felt she needed Adam, but he was too busy tending to Fanny. Adam felt Becky could handle herself and said he was just being polite to Fanny. But no matter how much he tried to reassure Becky, it seemed to make her madder and madder, until they weren't speaking. This was the first time they'd seen each other in a while.

"Go talk to him," Martha urged.

"I think I need another drink," Fanny said and went to push her way out of the corner to approach the bar. With the reflexes of a cobra, Becky snatched the glass out of Fanny's hand.

"I'll get it," Becky said before standing up and marching toward the bar.

Her red hair bounced around her face, and although she tried not to look directly at Adam, she couldn't miss him. He was wearing a tight vest buttoned over his work shirt. It made his shoulders look even wider. His work boots were dull compared to some of the gents' spit-shined spats. But Becky didn't care. She wouldn't care if he'd worn his bib overalls stained with ink from the press machines he worked on all the time. She thought he was the cat's pajamas, but she was not going to let him know that. Not if he insisted on giving Fanny the attention she wanted.

Becky wiggled her way between two fellows, one with a pencil-thin mustache and the other with a sparkling ruby ring on his pinky.

"Buy you a drink, doll?" Mr. Pinky Ring asked.

"Well, this actually isn't for me. It's for that dame over there." She pointed to Fanny.

Mr. Pinky Ring and Mr. Mustache nearly broke into a brawl deciding who would buy Fanny's next round. As they sashayed across the floor to deliver her champagne cocktail, Becky pretended not to notice Adam standing right next to her.

"Can I buy you a drink?" he asked.

"I don't know if I'm thirsty," she replied.

"Where have you been hiding yourself? I haven't seen you in a while."

"I'm not hiding. Maybe you just weren't really looking." Becky didn't want to snap at him. She wanted to kiss him. But her pride had taken up residence in her gut and was not willing to be evicted.

"Becky, I don't even know what I did. If you are jealous of Fanny and think that I'd..."

"I am not jealous of Fanny. I'm annoyed with Fanny. I'm tired of everyone tripping and falling all over themselves just to pick up a kerchief she blew her nose in," Becky snapped.

"So you want people to treat her as rudely as you do," Adam replied with a smirk. A couple loose black curls fell over his forehead when Becky looked up at him. How dare he look so handsome when she was seething at him? Who did he think he was?

"I don't know why I'm the only one who sees it. She is a snake like the one in God's garden." Becky looked over her shoulder to see that the two men who had brought her cousin a fresh cocktail were now flanking her, laughing and fawning all over her. And she knew that out of the corner of her eye, Fanny hadn't stopped watching her and Adam, calculating how she could undo anything Becky might put in place.

"You're not the only one, Becky." Adam sniffed. "Give me a little credit."

"Right." Becky harrumphed as she pointed to the ceiling. "If Fanny came over here and asked you to climb a ladder to fetch her one of those Chinese lanterns on the highest beam, you'd break your neck trying to do it for her."

"You think I'm that much of a pushover?" Adam replied.

"When it comes to her? Yes." Becky's gut twisted, and she instantly regretted saying anything. She should have just let Fanny come to the bar and get her own drink. She should have let her throw herself at Adam and just dealt with the consequences. If anyone was pushing Adam right into her clutches, it was Becky herself, and she was disgusted with herself for it.

"I guess you don't know me as well as I thought you did," Adam said.

"I guess I don't."

Adam downed the shot he had in front of him and ordered another.

"So, where does that leave us?"

"I'm not sure. I don't really have time to think about it right now," Becky said, biting her tongue to make sure she didn't start crying. She turned around and headed back to her table to snatch up her purse.

"Where are you going?" Fanny asked.

"Home," Becky said without any emotion.

"But Adam is here."

Becky looked at Fanny, who was looking at the bar, sizing Adam up.

"You wouldn't want anyone to scoop him out from under you." Fanny smirked and licked her lips.

"Tell Martha and Teddy I've left," Becky said.

"Hey, doll. What's your hurry? Wait for me, and I'll give you a lift," the man with the thin mustache said.

Becky hurried outside. Just as she was about to accept his offer she saw two people she knew.

"Delilah, Zachary? I almost didn't recognize you. Normally I see you two joined at the lips," Becky said, swallowing her emotions.

"I can't help it, Beck. She won't keep her hands off me," Zachary said, getting a giggle and a playful swat on the arm from Delilah.

"Hey, I got a shot of bad hooch. You think you can give me a ride?" Becky lied, but she couldn't just spill the fact that her heart was breaking and she was going to be a blubbering mess if she didn't get out of there.

"Sure. Want to join us for a bite to eat downtown?" Delilah offered.

As soon as Becky heard they were heading downtown, she had a better idea. "No thanks. But a lift downtown would be just what the doctor ordered."

She followed them to Zachary's car and hopped into the back seat. The conversation was all about the fire and the death of Mr. Ruthmeyer.

"I didn't know the man, but I heard he was very handsome," Delilah said.

"I'd only seen him on a couple of occasions. Each time, he was growling at someone about something. I don't think he and Mrs. Tobin were carrying on like people said," Zachary admitted. "He was too mean. That's why he was a bachelor. Couldn't find a decent woman who'd handcuff herself to him. What do you think, Beck? He lives just off your property."

"We never had any problems," Becky said as she watched the streetlights go by. "It was like we didn't know he was even there."

Zachary and Delilah continued chatting in the front seat. But it was obvious from the way Becky stared out into the darkness that she wasn't really listening. When they finally stopped the car, she hopped out.

"Thanks for the lift," Becky said, giving them each a hug.

"Are you sure you won't join us?" Delilah asked once more.

"No thank you. I've got to stop at the apothecary down the street. I've got a friend there who will take me home. If she can't, I'll flag down a cab." Becky waved cheerfully and hoped Delilah and Zachary wouldn't ask any more questions. Thankfully, they waved good-bye before wrapping their arms around one another and walking off to one of the all-night diners.

Becky headed in the opposite direction, thankful for the darkness and the shadows to hide the tears running down her cheeks. When she finally got to the apothecary, she was shocked to see so many people inside.

Madame Cecelia was there, as if she had been expecting Becky all night.

CHAPTER SIX

The apothecary numbered 784½ Bryn Mawr Street was jumping. Becky had never seen so many people in a drugstore in her whole life. Cecelia was behind the counter, wearing a lovely black dress with black fringe that shimmied with every move she made. Her ample bosom poured out the top and was the resting place for a huge green amber broach with a giant ant frozen in it.

"If you follow my instructions, you'll have no problems. I promise." Madame Cecelia spoke to an older man who couldn't have weighed more than eighty pounds. He had red cheeks and a nervous habit of tugging on his collar. She handed him a small paper bag that he took and quickly stuffed into his inside breast pocket. Then he handed over several dollars, slipped his hat back onto his head, gave Madame Cecelia a nervous smile, and earnestly exited the building.

"You look like you are swamped," Becky said. "I didn't mean to stop by and get in the way."

"Sure you did," Cecelia said, grinning.

"I didn't know where else to go." Saying those words let some air out of her. "I didn't want to go home. I didn't want to go to another joint. I'm feeling lost."

"Well, aren't you lucky. We specialize in finding lost things and setting them right. Go on upstairs. I'll be up shortly. There are some strange cookies Mama made if you are feeling adventurous."

"They aren't strange," hissed Ophelia, Cecelia's mother, as she scooted behind her daughter to grab some kind of salve in a jar from one of the higher shelves. The woman stood only a hair's breadth over four foot nine but had the aura of a prize-fighting pugilist.

Becky was happy for the invitation. She'd never thought she'd live to hear herself say she didn't want to go to another dive for a drink or a dance, but here she was at this bizarre store that attracted the most unusual customers at night, and she was thankful there was no bar.

The first time she had visited the store and gone upstairs, she had been bombarded by the specters of Cecelia's entire gypsy family. It had been an overwhelming experience that knocked her on her backside and had her stretched out on their couch in the tiny upstairs apartment, in need of smelling salts like a hysterical Southern belle. But after a few visits, Becky had learned that the spirits each had their place and could be addressed just like any flesh-and-bone folks. So with careful, slow steps, she ascended the staircase that wound around and around like a corkscrew, careful of the candles and smelly herbs placed in the corners.

The spirits had become accustomed to her and tipped their hats or curtsied or waved as she passed by. Except for Cousin Mimi. She scowled at Becky, called her names, and made rude gestures with her hands.

"She did that to everyone in life. Death hasn't changed her," Ophelia said with a sour grimace on her face.

Now Becky felt a certain kind of familiarity not just with Cecelia and her mother but with these spirits, too.

Of course, if her parents knew she was friends with the likes of gypsies, she would probably be sent to live in a convent. The thought made her think of Adam. He was a Northerner, which was just as bad as gypsies in the eyes of most home-grown Southerners. What was it about these societal outcasts that drew Becky to them?

She contemplated this as she gingerly stepped into the apartment. It was small, with white walls and a fire escape just outside the window. The window was open just a crack, and fresh, cool air was coming in. The entire house smelled of exotic incense that burned continually in front of a statue of the Virgin Mary holding the baby Jesus. But that was the only familiar thing in the place. Everything else—the pictures, the statues, and the knickknacks —was a jumble of curiosities that Becky loved to study with her artist's eye.

But tonight, she hadn't the desire to study their décor. She walked to the small kitchenette and saw the cookies Ophelia had been talking about. They were square things that looked like they had chocolate chips in them. Becky took one bite and realized they were not chocolate chips but dark, almost black dates. When her taste buds were expecting something comforting like chocolate and were instead slapped with the taste of a date, it made her entire body disappointed.

"Well, I can't put it back." Becky grimaced and took the cookie to the small table by the window and sat down.

It wasn't long before Cecelia came through the door, rolling her eyes. "My mother is begging for me to kill her," Cecelia said, removing the scarf from her thick black hair.

"What has she done?" Becky asked, swallowing the last of the cookie with great effort.

"Any male customer who comes in not wearing a wedding ring she's introducing me to. I'm busy with a lady who has a cyst in an uncomfortable place. I'm not looking for a husband. I'm looking for the medicine to help that go away. But Mama has to stop me in the middle of things to whisper in my ear, 'Mr. So-and-So has no wife. He believes in our customs. Shall I put a desire spell on him?'"

Becky laughed.

"Sure. It's funny to you. Mr. So-and-So needs powder because his feet itch and he can't hear out of his left ear. That's who she wants to marry me off to." Cecelia shook her head and flopped down in the seat across from Becky. "But I am so glad to see you. It seems like forever since we visited."

She took Becky's hands in hers and squeezed them. Becky looked up at Cecelia, and her smile quickly faded. Tears filled her eyes. She shook her head and pulled her hands back to cover her face.

"What?" Cecelia asked. "What is it? Oh, wait. Adam White."

Becky wailed and nodded her head. "I'm such a fool. I was horrible to him tonight. I don't know why. He was trying to be sweet, and what he was saying wasn't so awful, but...but..."

"Oh, dear. And you came here for comfort and had to eat one of Mama's burnt date cookies. Oh, that's from the frying pan into the fire."

"What's wrong with me, Cecelia?"

"The same thing wrong with all women in your condition. You are in love."

"Thanks. Brilliant insight. I can see the spirits are working double time for you." Becky chuckled.

"I will tell you this: Nothing pleases a man more than a woman apologizing to him. For some odd reason, that swells their chest and squares their shoulders more than a kiss. When you are wrong, say so with a sincere heart. He'll not be able to resist. And when you are right, apologize with a smirk."

"You're right. And I knew that. I guess I was just

hoping you'd offer to cast a spell on him. Maybe give him itchy feet for a few days."

The ladies chuckled together and continued talking as Cecelia put on a pot for tea.

"Please don't tell me you have tea that goes with these cookies." Becky frowned and stuck out her tongue.

"What's wrong with my cookies?" Ophelia asked. She'd come into the apartment without making a sound and made Becky jump like a cat.

"Well, Ophelia, they are an acquired taste, for sure. I haven't acquired that taste just yet," Becky stuttered. She liked Ophelia and didn't want to intentionally insult her or her cookies.

"You expected chocolate or something sweet?" Ophelia blinked. Even her white eye, which had been blinded long ago by cataracts, twinkled mischievously.

Becky nodded.

"That's what happens when you judge without knowing." And that was the end of that conversation. Ophelia disappeared back downstairs.

"You and your mother are on a real roll doling out the advice tonight. Yes, I'm so glad I came here in my time of need to get verbally slapped and have my taste buds assaulted. With friends like y'all…" Becky shook her head.

Cecelia laughed. "So tell me, what else is going on?" She poured the hot water into dainty teacups.

"Well, you heard about the fire? That seems to be on everyone's mind," Becky said, watching Cecelia's movements freeze as she stood in the tiny kitchenette.

"I heard something about a fire. I forget, Becky, do you take one lump or two with your tea?" Cecelia asked.

"No lumps. I take it straight," she joked. "You know that farm, the Ruthmeyer farm butts right up against my daddy's property? We were the first ones there, since I'd noticed the smoke from our parlor window."

Cecelia said nothing.

"I hate to admit that rushing off to help saved my ears from the horrible piano music being pounded out by my mother's guest. Like Ophelia, she wants me married off, too, and any man with prominent roots in the South will do."

Cecelia laughed a little too loudly but said nothing more.

"I swear, Cecelia, when we got there, I saw some very strange things. Poor Mr. Ruthmeyer was still alive and inside. The fire was in every window except the small attic room. That's where Mr. Ruthmeyer was. We all heard him screaming. It was…"

"Becky, I need you to stop talking about that." Cecelia whirled around and stared at her friend.

"What?"

Cecelia swallowed. "Please, for your own safety and mine, just forget about the fire, Mr. Ruthmeyer, the women. All of it."

"I didn't say anything about women," Becky replied slowly.

Cecelia let out a long sigh, and her back became rigid. She looked down at the tea she was preparing. A long silence passed between the women until Cecelia finally spoke.

"So you believe Mr. Ruthmeyer's death was a murder?"

"I'll say it's suspicious is all," Becky replied carefully. "There were a number of things that went on all at the same time while that fire was burning. I'm just saying that something doesn't seem on the level."

"My dear friend. Do you know what the Mafia is?" Cecelia asked.

"Darlin', I'm on a first-name basis with almost every bouncer at a good number of speakeasies all over Savannah. I think I've heard that term once or twice." She winked.

"This isn't funny. I'm not cracking wise," Cecelia said. "The Mafia is a church gathering compared to what Mr. Ruthmeyer was involved in. I am begging you, as your friend and someone who cares about you, to turn your back on this topic and never visit it again."

"How do you know so much?" Becky whispered.

"It comes with the territory." Cecelia waved her finger around the apartment and tapped the stack of tarot cards that were always on the kitchen table. "There are things going on with that piece of property and all the people involved that you don't want any part of. We aren't talking about an obsessed lover or even a person with a chip on their shoulder. This is much deeper. Becky, it's darker than you are prepared to deal with. Please, just forget about the fire."

"All right, Cecelia. I'll forget about it for now." Becky was more accustomed to ignoring advice than she ever was to heeding it.

Cecelia saw right through her. "I can't stop you from doing whatever cotton-headed thing you might be contemplating, but you've been warned." Cecelia shook her head.

The ladies chatted a little longer before Becky decided to head back home. She said good-bye to Cecelia after promising to be careful and waved good-bye to Ophelia, who was counselling an overweight woman about a mixture of spices and some strange rope that she was putting in a bag for her. Ophelia winked at Becky before she stepped out into the night air.

It was still early by Becky Mackenzie standards, and the hustle and bustle of the street seemed fresh and new again. So as any good soldier would do, she carried on and slipped into the first gin joint she could find. There were a few familiar faces that happily whirled her around the dance floor. The bartender was a friend of a friend and slipped her two shots on the house.

By the time she was ready to leave, she was feeling much better than she had been at Willie's. But the instruction Cecelia had given her regarding Adam sounded about right. Yet who wanted to eat so much crow? And why didn't he feel the least bit bad for putting her in such a predicament? Why did everyone think that Fanny Doshoffer was some kind of class act when she was no better than an alley cat? Was it just because she had gone to France?

"The Marquis de Sade was from France. I don't

see anyone making excuses for him," Becky muttered as she walked down the sidewalk. Her voice drew the attention of more than one couple as they passed her. "What are you looking at? Never saw a woman talk to herself before?"

This walking was never going to cut it. Becky hailed a cab and, with the few cents she had left, had them drop her at the entrance of the Old Brick Cemetery. She'd be home in no time if she didn't mind cutting through the tombstones. Normally, she didn't. Tonight was no exception—or so she thought until she realized she wasn't the only one in the cemetery.

CHAPTER SEVEN

"*A*re you sure you want me to drop you off here?" the cabdriver asked nervously, looking at the rickety gate and dilapidated wrought iron fence. "Looks a little desolate. A young lady shouldn't be roaming through those graves by herself. Or at all."

Becky chuckled. "My daddy's house is just on the other side. By the time you drive all around and pull up our long dirt road, I'll be in bed fast asleep. But I do appreciate your kindness."

"All right, ma'am. Be careful." He tipped his hat after Becky handed him his money and tip before waving him on.

She'd crossed the cemetery more often than she cared to admit. Had Kitty known how often she crossed this sacred ground, she would have gasped and demanded that Judge pay to have a new gate and fence put up around the entire bone yard just so she wouldn't be able to take the ghoulish shortcut. Becky understood why most people would shudder at the thought of creeping along the overgrown paths at night with nothing more than the moonlight to guide them. It was the only place where the living could be literally alone yet completely surrounded by other people. But Becky knew she wasn't alone and had several ghostly chaperones to escort her safely to her father's property.

But tonight, she would have been hard-pressed not to notice that none of her usual traveling companions had come to greet her. Mr. Wilcox was her favorite. He was a pleasant old man who bragged about his eleven grandchildren and cracked wise about his wife of thirty-three years. Hardly a week went by when she didn't see him at least twice. But he was nowhere to be found. As Becky proceeded along her usual route, she noticed that not only were her deceased friends not around, but neither were the usual nighttime creatures. There was no hoot of the great horned owls that took up residence in oak trees, nor were field mice or raccoons kicking up the brush. In fact, now that Becky was paying attention, she didn't so much as feel the tickle of a moth against her skin or hear the buzz of a mosquito in her ear. Something was wrong.

As she kept walking, she felt a shift in the air. The quiet became heavy, and although she could see nothing out of place, it was as if she was seeing the landscape for the first time. And for the first time, she felt as if the landscape was seeing her.

Before she came to the turn in the path that started her in the direction of her home, Becky finally heard something. At first she thought maybe a screech owl was calling for its mate. They didn't always cry out in wild shrieks. Those stoic birds uttered the most adorable chirps when they were feeling romantic. But this wasn't that adorable sound. It was sobbing. A child was crying close by.

In the bright moonlight, Becky followed the sound and saw the faint image of a little girl kneeling on the ground. Her hair was long and waved in a breeze Becky couldn't feel. She was wearing a simple gunnysack dress. Becky couldn't see her feet—not because they were covered but because they weren't there.

"Honey? Why are you crying?" Becky whispered as she slowly approached the girl.

"They're disturbing the old folks." The girl's voice

was soft. "Why would they do such a thing to them? They just want to lie in peace."

Becky assumed the girl was talking about something in her short life that had left a deep impression. But as she got nearer to her, she realized she had seen her before. Her name was Eugenia, and she'd died of fever during the War of Northern Aggression.

"Eugenia, honey, who are you talking about? You know your family is waiting for you. They aren't disturbed," Becky soothed.

"They are too disturbed. They're stealing their soil and disturbing them. Why would they do that? Those old folks never did anything to them. It's cruel, I tell you." She sobbed uncontrollably.

Becky knew what to do when a child cried. How many times had she comforted Teeter when he'd hit a rough patch or taken a spill? So many times she'd lost count. She'd take him in her arms and rock him and tell him something sweet while smoothing his soft hair. The urge to do the same for Eugenia took hold of Becky, but as soon as she stepped closer, the girl faded into almost nothing. Her little face looked horrified and woeful all at once.

"Don't worry, honey. It'll be okay."

"Will you stop them from stealing their dirt? Will

you make them stop digging? Please promise you'll make them stop," Eugenia pleaded.

"I promise." Becky didn't know what else to say. "I'll make them stop."

Eugenia seemed to accept this as she wiped her nose on the back of her arm and then looked over her shoulder. She stood up and pointed, and just like a wisp of smoke out the top of a chimney, she was gone.

Suddenly the hairs on the back of Becky's neck stood up. She looked in the direction Eugenia had pointed. Off in the distance was a small light. It was swinging back and forth, but it didn't appear to be advancing. Feeling rather territorial and offended that someone else would be walking in what she considered *her* cemetery, Becky carefully began to inch her way toward the swinging light.

Without any other sounds of nature, she was sure she heard a low female voice whispering something along with the sound of shovels hitting dirt—two of them if she was hearing clearly.

Careful not to give herself away, Becky stepped off the weed-covered path and slipped into the shadows of the tombstones. The blankets of moss hanging from the trees hid her from the moonlight. When she'd crept as far as she could without being seen, Becky peeked from behind a tall tombstone so worn and weathered that the names and dates were nothing more than cracks and dents in the stone. As she got down on her knees and squinted in the direction of the lamp, her breath caught in her throat. It was the woman from the fire. Not Mrs. Tobin but the other woman. Her skin looked oily in the yellow light. Her hair was concealed beneath the purple wrap on her head. She was muttering something as two men continued to dig the dirt. They looked as if they hadn't eaten in weeks and were nothing more than muscle, skin, and bones. Their skin shined like slick oil in the tiny light, too.

Were they slaves? Was this woman working them to death? And why was she in the cemetery?

Carefully, Becky started to creep closer. The next tombstone was a few feet away beneath a heavily mossed bough. She crawled on her hands and knees, barely feeling the earth and pebbles that dug into her flesh.

Soon she was safely concealed behind another tombstone that was nothing more than a worn-down arch that looked like a jagged tooth in a hobo's mouth. Becky was almost on her belly as she peered around the side.

It looked as if the woman in the head wrap was in

some kind of trance. She stood dangerously close to the edge of the hole the two men were digging, swaying as she muttered words Becky couldn't understand. How was she hanging like that? How did she manage not to fall into the grave face-first?

How Hugh Loomis was able to remain standing after drinking moonshine is a complete mystery, too. The world is full of them, she thought.

Suddenly the woman's head snapped up and twisted unnaturally in Becky's direction while her feet remained firmly planted at the very edge of the hole. Becky looked into her eyes and was sure they were all white. Within a split second, they snapped back to what eyes were supposed to look like, and she muttered something unintelligible. Whatever it was, the two men stopped digging. With the agility of cats, both men hopped out of the hole and began walking in Becky's direction. If she stayed where she was, there was a good chance they'd see her. She could play drunk, pretend she was in dreamland and stumbling home when she crossed their path. But drunks disappeared all the time. It was a rare occasion, but it did happen that some poor rummy would fall asleep with his head on the train tracks, only to wake up at the Pearly Gates after the train ran over him. She could hold her breath and stay as still as a statue and hope they wouldn't see her.

Just as Becky was deciding to stay put, a shaft of moonlight hit both their faces.

They looked like something out of a nightmare. From a distance, they looked like ordinary men. Thin, yes. But still, they looked like men who Becky might see walking down the street or even asking to work in her father's tobacco fields. But there was something missing. They were in a trance. Their eyes had rolled over white. Not like Ophelia's white, cataract-filled eye but white as if the irises were missing. How did they see to dig, to walk, to search for her? They were being led, and Becky felt it was by a force that wasn't their own will.

She pressed her body so close and flat to the ground that her own breath, as quiet and shallow as it was, bounced back from the dirt up against her chin. She didn't dare move. The whispers from the woman echoed in the empty graveyard and were answered with grunts and gurgles from her two assistants. As Becky focused on their expressionless faces, a new revelation jumped out at her so viciously she almost screamed.

Their mouths were sewn shut.

Becky's breath hitched in her throat. Both men

looked in her direction. Without waiting, Becky jumped up and took off running through the dark cemetery. She was sure each footfall was like a gong going off, giving away her position. She made it to the halfway point before stopping behind a wide oak tree whose branches stretched out like long arms. Her chest was heaving, and she was drenched in sweat. Her dress was ruined, she was sure, and her shoes would be tossed into the garbage as soon as Kitty saw them. But Kitty's wrath was the least of her worries.

Carefully, she peeked around the tree. The men were getting closer. But their steps were clumsy and unsteady. They didn't know the cemetery like Becky did. Slowly, Becky bent down. Gingerly, she felt around until her fingers felt the cool, smooth texture of a stone. She dug her nails around it, picked it up, and with all her might threw it back in the direction she'd come. The men, if she could call them that, whirled around and stumbled in the direction of the noise.

Becky took off running in the opposite direction. Never before had she wished for the end of the cemetery to come quickly. Of all the places she visited, it was this poor old bone yard that had brought her the most joy, the most peace. And now someone and a couple of some*things* had inserted themselves into this peaceful place and made it unfamiliar and scary.

Becky didn't look back. Not until she was safely inside the tobacco field did she turn around. The tobacco was almost taller than Becky's head, but she could still, on tiptoes, see over the top. No one was following her. But she got the worst feeling that that didn't mean someone wasn't watching her. The sweet smell of the rows of tobacco brought her a feeling of comfort that she was almost home. She slowed her pace a little and tried to catch her breath.

When Becky reached the clearing and was just a stone's throw from her house, she heard the words on the wind, and they hit her ears like nails on a chalkboard.

"You saw the fire."

CHAPTER EIGHT

*T*hat night Becky found it nearly impossible to sleep. She'd shinnied up the trellis outside her window to avoid a chance encounter with her mother. She wasn't sure which was worse, the woman with the head wrap or Kitty catching a glimpse of her in her ruined dress and shoes. After washing up and trying to figure out what it really was that she had seen, she gave up and just propped her vanity chair in front of the window and watched the darkness.

Part of her was terrified that a fire might start in Daddy's tobacco field. If whoever was messing around in the graveyard had anything to do with the fire at Mr. Ruthmeyer's, they had made it clear that burning a man alive made no difference to them.

What did a couple thousand acres of tobacco mean? But as Becky watched with wide, dry eyes, she saw nothing. She was tired. Exhausted. But the minute she tried to lie down, she saw those men with the stitches over their mouths and that woman in the head wrap leaning over that open grave.

Whatever they were doing was sacrilege. During her visits, Becky might have accidentally walked over a couple graves or spilled a glass of sweet tea, but she would never think of disturbing those laid to rest by digging, scratching, or otherwise altering their final resting places. Visiting the dead was a gesture of kindness. Spoiling their graves was an act of evil. And whoever had found the Old Brick Cemetery thought they could claim squatter's rights.

Finally, as the sun was coming up, Becky crawled into her bed and fell into a deep sleep. She didn't dream, but she jumped out of her skin when Fanny came barging in calling her name.

"What happened to you? You look like something the cat dragged in," Fanny said as if she hadn't instigated more hard feelings between the two of them.

"Nothing," Becky muttered before rubbing her face. "When did you get home?"

"Oh, it had to be around one, maybe two. After you left, Willie's seemed to come alive. The drinks were flowing, and the beaus were lining up to dance. It was a grand time," Fanny gushed.

"That's funny. I thought I was awake at that time," Becky muttered. She looked at her chair, which was still in front of her window, and swallowed hard. Obviously she'd drifted off before Teddy brought Fanny home and hadn't heard his boiler when it pulled up. But stranger things than that had happened.

"Well, Aunt Kitty told me to wake you up. We're going into town." Fanny put her hand on her hip. "She says you need a new frock or something for a visitor that will be coming within the next few weeks."

"Visitor? Who?"

"Beats me. She said he is the cousin of Lucille and will be visiting Savannah within the next few weeks and will be looking for someone to show him around town." Fanny batted her eyes.

It was obvious to Becky that Fanny was already plotting how to insert herself into any meeting Becky was going to have with a member of the opposite sex. Why didn't her mother just fix Fanny up?

"Not another one," Becky groaned, flopping back down on her bed.

"The shops in Savannah aren't nearly as quaint as they are in Paris, but the sizes do run larger here. Lucky for you," Fanny chuckled.

"Is there anything else?" Becky snapped.

"Just that Aunt Kitty said to hurry." Fanny took a step out the door before turning and leaning on the knob. "Oh, and Mr. White told me to tell you he sends his regards. He is a divine dancer. You feel like your feet don't even touch the ground when you're in his arms."

Becky's mouth went dry as her eyes flooded with tears. The last thing she wanted to do was go out with Fanny or her mother and have them both telling her how she could be just as pretty as so-and-so or she'd be more popular if she just did such-and-such. She was a one-legged man in a keister-kicking contest.

She had stripped out of her clothes the previous night, and there was still some dirt beneath her fingernails. She hurried into the bathroom, filled the sink, and washed herself up. Her hair was a wild, unruly red mess.

"*Of course* I'm a mess today," she said to her reflection in her hand mirror. "I'm going out with my mother and Fanny. I *have* to look like Quasimodo."

Then she looked down and saw her knees. They were still black with dirt and scratched as if she'd been dragged through the cemetery instead of running through it. Quickly she hopped up onto the bathroom vanity and stuck her feet in the sink. Even after she'd cleaned herself off from head to toe, her knees still looked like they had when she was twelve and constantly crawling around outside, digging up worms or studying ant hills or playing hide-and-seek with Teddy.

"What I wouldn't give to play a game of hide-and-seek right now," Becky muttered. "I'd hide from Fanny all day."

"Rebecca Madeline MacKenzie! You get yourself downstairs this instant!" her mother shouted up the stairs.

Just then, there was a gentle rap on the door. Becky hopped off the vanity and, dripping water on the floor, opened the door a crack. To her great relief, it was Lucretia. She had a cup of steaming coffee in one hand and a wedge of cornbread in the other.

"Miss Fanny's been making a point to dump out the coffee early if you ain't had none yet, and poor Moxley nearly lost his hand trying to swipe you this last slice from her before she could force it down,"

Lucretia whispered. "That gal don't know we're on to her."

"Oh, thanks, Lucy. You are just top drawer," Becky said softly.

"Leave the dishes in your room. I'll pick them up later." She winked and hurried down the back steps that led around to the kitchen.

Quickly, Becky slurped the hot coffee and gobbled up the cornbread. Normally, she would have wiped a huge pat of butter on Lucretia's already moist cornbread, but beggars couldn't be choosers.

"I'm coming, Mama!" she yelled as she tip-toed back into her room and shut the door. When she finally emerged, she was feeling much better about things.

"What are you wearing?" Kitty asked, looking Becky up and down.

"What's the matter?" Becky smirked.

"Ladies in the North might wear trousers, but here in Savannah, a lady wears a skirt when she's out at midday," Kitty huffed.

"Why, Mama. I was just perusing one of Cousin Fanny's French couture magazines and saw that trousers were all the rage in Paris. I don't think a million Parisians can be wrong." Becky tittered. "Isn't that right, Fanny?"

Kitty whirled around and stared at her niece.

"Uh, well, it is common for some of the less fortunate women to be seen in slacks." Fanny cleared her throat. "It is rather common, I suppose."

"What is the world coming to?" Kitty shook her head and, clutching her purse, exited the house. Fanny followed closely behind as Becky brought up the rear at a casual stroll. As soon as she got into the car, she pulled out a fedora she'd bought ages ago and had yet to wear. It covered her unruly hair and drove both Fanny and her mother crazy.

"It seems we are just in time to find you a new wardrobe." Kitty exhaled. "No daughter of mine is going to look like a man. I don't care what they're wearing in Paris."

Becky could have kissed her mama for uttering those words. But instead, she relaxed in the back seat and tried to figure out what she'd seen and heard the night before. More importantly, what was she going to do about it?

CHAPTER NINE

*A*s the trio were walking down the bustling sidewalk in downtown Savannah, Fanny kept up a constant dialogue with Kitty about her vast knowledge of French cuisine.

"Don't get me wrong, Aunt Kitty. I love fried chicken and grits as much as the next girl. But there is something about a baguette with brie and strawberries on a summer afternoon at an outdoor café in Paris that screams culture."

"You would be the expert on that," Kitty replied. "None of us have any reason to cross the ocean. However, if Becky ever wanted to, I know her daddy and I would be happy to send her anywhere she might like to go. So long as she was chaperoned."

Becky chuckled but said nothing. As she let

Fanny and Kitty talk, she couldn't help but count how many blocks she was away from Adam's newspaper presses. He'd be hard at work right now. Maybe hanging around outside with his pals with his overalls rolled down to his waist while he drank a Coke in the alley or had a cigarette. His hair would be tousled and hanging in loose curls across his forehead. Oh, how she hated him for being so adorable. And the nerve of him dancing with Fanny! Of all the dames he could cut the rug with, he chose her.

It had to be for spite. He was mad at you. Just do what Cecelia said. Apologize. You know Fanny isn't half the woman you are.

As Becky thought that thought, a row of fellows conversing on the corner stopped what they were doing to watch Fanny walk by. It was the odd man out, wearing glasses so thick and a bow tie nearly devoured by his second chin, who winked at Becky. She couldn't help herself. She winked back and chuckled.

Heck, he could be a great dancer and maybe knows his way around the dives in town, she thought. *And there is the real difference between you and Fanny. The difference that Adam sees, that Martha and Teddy see, that Cecelia sees. You are a good egg. There's just no denying it.*

Her internal pep talk made Becky smile and lift

her chin to look at all the folks on the street. Just as she did, she saw Mrs. Tobin. She was carrying a small paper bag and hurrying down an alley, looking all around her as if she were afraid she was being followed. She was wearing a long coat for such a pleasant day. Becky's first thought was that Mr. Tobin had worked her over.

"I think I just saw Martha and her mother," Becky lied. "I'll catch up with you at Maxwell's for lunch."

"All right, darling," Kitty said.

"Be sure to give Martha my love," Fanny quipped. "We did have such a fine time last night after you left."

"You left Martha last night?" Kitty asked. "What in the world for?"

"I had a real pain," Becky replied, looking at Fanny. "I'll see you at lunch."

Without waiting for another word, Becky hurried off toward the alley where she was sure she had seen Mrs. Tobin.

As Becky rounded the corner, she saw the woman hurrying along. It was a sunny day, but the sun never reached its fingers between the two brick buildings. The alley was lined with bricked-up windows and doors that had either clunky padlocks on them or wooden planks nailed across them.

Long, thin gutters ran from the roofs all the way down to empty on the cobblestone street, which made the shape of a V so the water wouldn't collect and instead found its way to run down the sewer grates.

Becky wobbled slightly, as the sloped street surface was tricky to maneuver. She kept her distance as she tailed the woman who, just three short days ago, looked to have been ripped in two with grief. Now she looked like she was on a very serious mission that required she wear a long coat that covered her from chin to shin.

Just before Becky was sure Mrs. Tobin was going to slip into the foot traffic on the next street over, the woman slipped into a dark, narrow gangway and pounded on the door. When the door opened, a man with hairy arms, wearing a sleeveless undershirt, tan trousers, and a fedora, stepped out.

From Becky's angle, it looked like Mrs. Tobin was flashing whatever she was hiding underneath that coat. But before any unsavory images came to her mind, Becky saw the man take a flask the size of the Holy Bible from under Mrs. Tobin's jacket. He reached into his pocket, pulled out a wad of money, and handed it to her. With no more than a nod, Mrs.

Tobin was hurrying in Becky's direction, buttoning up her overcoat.

Becky pressed her back against the wall and waited for the woman to pass. As soon as she did, Becky followed her again. Once they were both on the busy sidewalk, Becky inched up closer and closer behind her. Finally she reached out and tapped her on the shoulder.

Mrs. Tobin's face contorted into a frightened grimace when she turned around.

"Yes, can I help you?" she snapped.

She looked much different from the agonized woman Becky had seen the other day. She wasn't what the gents would call a ripe tomato, but she had striking, distinctive features. Her thin nose drew a long line down the middle of her face. Over the bridge were dainty freckles that matched her brown hair. Her cheekbones were high, giving her face a thin, elegant look that went with the rest of her delicate frame. Her wrists were thin, as were her ankles. If she was carrying hooch around in giant flasks, she had to be a lot stronger than she appeared.

"I wanted to offer you my condolences," Becky said.

"Condolences? For what?"

"I was at the fire at Mr. Ruthmeyer's house. My

father helped put the fire out," Becky replied. "It looked like he meant a lot to you."

"Yeah, so what's that to you?"

"It's nothing to me. I just wanted to say I was sorry for you." Becky watched her reaction.

Truthfully, Becky didn't want to hurt the woman or embarrass her or even question her. She had just felt so genuinely bad for her that she wanted to say something. Plus, had she actually been having an affair with John Ruthmeyer, she might be in trouble from the people who had burned his house down. She might be in trouble with her husband. It was not uncommon for a man to take his belt to his wife for such an indiscretion. Becky tried to see if Mrs. Tobin had any such marks. If she did, they were well hidden.

"Look, I don't know you from a hole in the ground. But let me give you some friendly advice. Don't go sticking your nose where it doesn't belong." She pointed one of her long, bony, elegant fingers at Becky.

"Why are you running hooch under your coat?"

"What? I'm doing no such thing," Mrs. Tobin said quietly while looking around.

"Who was that woman with you at the fire? The

woman with the purple wrap around her head?" Becky pushed.

Those words were like shards of ice down Mrs. Tobin's back. She frowned and shivered.

"I'm trying to be as polite as possible. Mind your own business."

She turned to leave, but Becky took hold of her arm. Becky wasn't that big herself but her hand completely encircled Mrs. Tobin's arm. She could feel her muscles tighten beneath the material of her coat.

"That makes two of us. Mrs. Tobin, I saw you crying at the sight of Mr. Ruthmeyer's house on fire. I saw that woman in the head scarf arrive, and you stopped and went off with her. Who is she? Why would you go with her and not stay to help the man…"

"Stay and help John Ruthmeyer?" she hissed. "Stay and help the man who ruined my life? There are things that go on on these country roads that you don't know about, girlie-girl," Mrs. Tobin said.

That was the second time someone had called Becky girlie-girl. The first had been at the dive with the moonshine, and the gent who'd said it did so with the same contempt as Mrs. Tobin.

"What kind of things? Who was that woman?" Becky asked bravely.

"That woman is my housekeeper. She's been with my husband's family for over three decades. When we married, she came with us. That's all." Mrs. Tobin began to tremble and look around nervously.

"Is she here in the city with you?" Becky pushed.

"You seem like a very nice girl. I'm sorry if I was short with you, but please do as I say and don't ask any more questions." Mrs. Tobin was starting to get flustered.

"Mrs. Tobin, my name is Becky Mackenzie. My father's tobacco farm was right against Mr. Ruthmeyer's homestead. Daddy never had a dispute with Mr. Ruthmeyer. He never had a negative thing to say about the man. In my book, that makes him a good egg. If there is something you know about that fire, you can tell me, and I'll help…"

Mrs. Ruthmeyer's eyes began to water. Her bottom lip started to tremble, and she was clenching her jaw as if chewing the words before they came out would prevent her from saying anything.

"You can't help me. You can't help either one of us. If anyone saw us together, I don't want to think of what could happen. Now please, before someone sees you," Mrs. Tobin urged.

"Mrs. Tobin, I'll be having lunch with my mother at Maxwell's at noon. If you want to get me a message, you'll find me there," Becky said. "You aren't alone, Mrs. Tobin."

For a second, Mrs. Tobin looked at Becky as if she wanted to start talking and never stop. But no words came out. She parted her lips, but nothing happened. Just when Becky thought she was going to spill the beans, Mrs. Tobin became angry.

"I know what you are. You're just a busybody. I don't see a ring on your finger. You don't know what it takes to make a man happy and keep a household running," Mrs. Tobin said, lifting her chin.

"What?"

"A wife does what she has to in order to keep the wolves from the door. You'd do well to remember that if you ever find some halfwit to marry the likes of you. Now I'll thank you to leave me alone." With that, Mrs. Tobin was off and lost in the lunchtime crowd.

Feeling like she had snapped a piece of the puzzle into place only to realize she'd lost a separate piece along the way, Becky headed for Maxwell's. She hadn't had anything but that wedge of cornbread since her ordeal the night before, and her stomach was growling and fussing to beat the band. When she stepped into the restaurant, Becky was instantly greeted by the maître d', Mr. Linus Morrell.

"Hello, Miss Rebecca. My, you are looking lovely today," he said, offering her his elbow. "Your mother and cousin are waiting for you."

"Thanks, Linus. Hey, you wouldn't want to whisk me away to Willie's for a couple of spins around the dance floor instead of sitting with my cousin for lunch, would you?" Becky whispered in Linus's ear. She'd seen him more than once at Willie's, always with a different girl on his arm, always with a big fat cigar.

"You know I would, but I've got to work," Linus replied. He was old enough to be Becky's father, but he enjoyed an innocent flirt nonetheless. "There you go breaking my heart. Well, maybe next time."

Becky squeezed his arm before letting go and sauntering up to her mother and Fanny. They were seated at a table right smack in the middle of the room.

"What happened to our window seat?" Becky asked. Normally when she came to downtown Savannah with her mama, they would have lunch at Maxwell's, sitting by the window to watch the people go by.

"Fanny said she was feeling a little head heavy

and thought the sun shining on her might aggravate her condition," Kitty answered. "It was the only seat available. Had I known you were going to dress the way you have today, I might have suggested a table in the far corner. As it is, several of the ladies of the Women's Auxiliary are here and have already taken notice of us."

"Aside from all that, I am famished," Becky said, ignoring her mother. "I think I might just order myself some fried chicken. All Fanny's talk about it has made me grow a craving the size of a catcher's mitt."

"Don't you dare!" Kitty gasped. "Fanny was just telling me about how they frown on such things in Paris like eating poultry with your fingers. I don't think they even serve fried chicken here."

"I was just joking, Mama." Becky shook her head. "I'm going to get my usual: tomato soup and crab cakes."

"As I was telling Aunt Kitty, at the restaurants in Paris, it is offensive to leave a tip of any kind. They find us Americans truly silly for such a tradition."

Fanny continued talking, although Becky wasn't paying particular attention. She wasn't being rude. That would do nothing except upset her mother. But suddenly Becky became keenly aware of what Fanny was saying.

"I wouldn't turn around to look, but this woman has just walked in wearing a long coat that is completely out of season. Now, if she were in Paris, I doubt anyone at any respectable café would seat her. You just don't do things like that."

Becky had her back to the entrance and didn't dare turn around. But she was sure that was the description of Mrs. Tobin. Was it really possible that two women were traipsing around town in long, heavy coats when it was a comfortable seventy-five degrees outside?

"Oh, I do believe I see Mrs. Penbroke with her husband. I just must say hello. Fanny, have you met the Penbrokes?" Kitty asked. "They just adore Becky. Why, Mrs. Penbroke thinks she'd make a fine wife and mother and has joked how terribly wonderful it would be if she were to settle down with one of their kin. We'd be related." Kitty giggled.

"Mama, have you been drinking?" Becky asked.

"I'm going to go and say hello," Kitty said, pushing away from the table.

"May I join you?" Fanny asked. Of course she'd want to meet the Penbrokes. Who wouldn't? After all, if they adored Becky, they'd just explode with hysterical fits of passion for Fanny.

"Are you coming?" Kitty asked Becky.

"I'll be there in just a moment, Mama. I think I have a snag in my trousers."

Becky smiled awkwardly as her mother rolled her eyes and walked across the restaurant. All eyes were on Fanny. She made sure of that by swinging her hips like a pendulum. Becky could have ripped her trousers completely up the back, exposing her bloomers for the world to see, and no one would notice if Fanny were within ten feet of her.

"Miss Becky." It was Linus. "A young lady asked me to give you this note. She wouldn't stay or give her name." He handed Becky a small, folded piece of paper. Inside was a warning.

The fire was just for show. It wasn't an accident. But I'm afraid of what we've started. Don't go near the rubble. Stay away from it, me, and everything.

If Mrs. Tobin thought her message would deter Becky from helping her, she was wrong. Now Becky was determined to check out not only the site of the fire but Mrs. Tobin's homestead, too.

CHAPTER TEN

After arriving home from a grueling day of playing nice with Cousin Fanny just for Mama's sake, Becky felt as if she'd swum the length of the Mississippi River. Her shoulders ached, her legs were like lead, and all she wanted was to rest in the quiet of her room. The idea of going out that night didn't even appeal to her, especially if Fanny was going to be tagging along. Of course she wanted to see Adam, but the thought of him twirling a swooning, clinging Fanny Doshoffer in his arms made Becky shudder. How could he be so easily taken in by her when he had such a good head on his shoulders otherwise?

"Oh, I can't think about it anymore. I'll give myself a case of hives," Becky grumbled as she pushed open her bedroom door and proceeded to flop down and sink a good three inches into her down comforter. Her entire body relaxed. She could have lain there for days.

"Knock-knock." Fanny poked her head in.

Becky cursed her absentmindedness for not shutting the door. "Yes, Fanny?"

"I was just curious if you knew what plans there were for this evening? I was going to wear my new dress if you thought the occasion was special enough." Fanny had purchased a bright-pink number that shimmered with every step. It was pretty and looked wonderful on her. Becky hated it.

"I think you'll be on your own. I'm happy right where I am," Becky replied, closing her eyes.

"Oh, I do hope you haven't decided to pull yourself up tight like a little clam on account of me dancing with Adam last night?" Fanny pouted.

Becky's eyes popped open, and she looked at her cousin but said nothing.

"He just wouldn't take no for an answer."

"That's fine, Fanny." Becky closed her eyes again and folded her hands over her stomach as if she were lying in a casket for final viewing. All she needed was her rosary beads woven through her fingers.

"So you aren't going out this evening?" Fanny prodded.

"Nope." Becky thought she was telling enough of the truth to satisfy her cousin. Actually, Becky had plans to go out, but if Fanny thought the Crazy Calico was too rough and real, she certainly would have no desire to go to the ashy remains of the Ruthmeyer homestead or hop down a few miles to the Tobin farm.

It was well after eleven when Becky shinnied down the trellis wearing her slacks, a heavy sweater, and her hat to keep her disguised as well as warm. The temperature had dropped. It was a rare occurrence to have such a cold night before tobacco harvesting had started. Her breath came out in little plumes of steam as she took the same dirt road that Hugh Loomis had driven down when they first saw the smoke above the trees.

Thankfully, unlike the other night in the cemetery, all the creatures of the night were conducting their routine symphony. Crickets chirped to each other across the grass. High in the trees, the hoot owls serenaded the moon. Had she not been going to the scene of a grisly death, this would have been a lovely walk.

By the time she reached the remains of the Ruthmeyer house, she was sweating. There was nothing left of the structure except some beams and part of the front porch steps. In the small bit of light coming from the half moon, Becky could see some pipes jutting out of the foundation and what looked like a sink. There was also a good number of what looked like metal washtubs. They were blackened and bent, but there were quite a number of them. Why would anyone need so many washtubs?

"Of course. He was brewing his own hooch," Becky said while snapping her fingers. "That's the only reason anyone would have that many washtubs. And from the looks of it, you were a very busy man, Mr. Ruthmeyer. This many tubs could make a man a very pretty penny. Or get him in trouble with the already established rum runners."

Becky decided she'd seen enough. There wouldn't be any further digging into this death by the police. It was sure to have already been ruled just an unfortunate accident. What did the police care if one low-level bootlegger got burned alive? That was one less bootlegger they'd have to chase down. If an "accident" made their job easier, all the better.

Now that she had stopped walking, Becky was starting to feel a chill creep over her shoulders. Without lingering any longer at the Ruthmeyer property, she headed in the direction of the Tobins' homestead.

Just the way Judge Mackenzie's tobacco fields butted against John Ruthmeyer's property, so did the Ruthmeyer property butt up against the Tobin property. The property lines were divided by a fence at the furthest end of the plot. It was no different from Judge's fence. But unlike the relationship of mutual respect between Judge Mackenzie and Mr. Ruthmeyer, Mr. Tobin and Mr. Ruthmeyer were sworn enemies. Why? No one knew for sure—except maybe Mrs. Tobin.

Becky couldn't stay on the road all the way to the Tobin farm without being seen from a dozen different angles. The house was built on a hill, surrounded by some rather unruly scrub and dense trees. By the time Becky reached a place where she could see the house clearly, she was sweating again. In order to maneuver silently through the trees and tall grass, Becky moved slowly. Reaching for the thin trees and using them for balance before taking a step made the procedure painfully tedious but as silent as snow falling.

More than likely, inside the house, there was a shotgun by both the front door and the back. A man who lived on a piece of property like this was ready to confront any trespassers. He'd be completely within his rights to shoot first and ask questions later.

Still, Becky was worried about Mrs. Tobin. She was afraid that Mr. Tobin was going to do to her the same thing he had done to Ruthmeyer.

But you don't know he did anything. You don't know he had anything to do with it. Just because they didn't like each other, just because there were rumors floating around doesn't convict a man of murder.

Becky shook her head. What was she doing out here? This was the craziest idea she'd had in...well, at least a couple weeks.

Finally, panting and sweating, she made it to a tall pile of kindling that was just a few short paces from the house. Crouching in its shadow, she was able to get a good look inside through the opened windows.

It was a huge house, with three levels including the attic. But from what Becky could see through the open windows, there were no pictures or wallpaper on the walls. It was as drab as could be. Becky thought going to sleep and waking up in that dreary place had to be a continual heartbreak. If it were her, she'd risk a beating to paint the walls bright red. But then she remembered she wasn't there to offer any kind of interior design advice. It was Mrs. Tobin Becky was concerned with.

After taking a deep breath and holding it, Becky darted toward the house. She reached the side of the front porch and waited. Only when she was sure no one had seen her did she slowly let her breath out. The porch light was no greater than that of a candle.

The smell hit her first. It was a pungent smell of maybe garlic, maybe onions in with something she didn't dare consider lingering behind it all. As she looked through the slats in the porch fence, she saw a couple of mason jars. Some were filled with clear liquid and reminded Becky of the moonshine Hugh had been drinking. Others were filled with something foul that Becky didn't even want to guess at. Why would anyone have that on their porch? Unless they wanted to make sure no visitors or snake-oil salesmen paid them a visit.

With her hand over her nose, Becky slipped along the side of the house. Taking just a few steps, she reached the cellar doors and was below what she assumed was the kitchen window. She froze as she heard someone clanging pots and pans around. Why would they be cooking at this late hour? In fact, why were so many of the lights on in the house?

"What are you doing?" a female voice hissed.

Becky froze.

"I'm going to check the generator," a man snapped back.

"The generator's fine."

"It's my house! If I want to check the generator, I'll check the generator!"

Suddenly Becky regretted not doing what Mrs. Tobin had instructed. What was she doing out here? Mr. Tobin would kill her if he saw her. She was frozen, pressed up against the house and listening to the man scream at his wife.

"Is this your house?" the woman taunted.

Just then, Becky heard something she'd never forget. Mr. Tobin started weeping. He began to apologize, to stutter and trip all over his words as if his tongue was being held between two fingers.

"There there, boy. Haven't I taken care of you this far? Do you think I won't take care of you until I die? Or until *you* die?" She chuckled sadistically.

Mr. Tobin said yes over and over. He said he loved her and trusted her and always would. He was hardly the masher Becky had been sure she was going to discover. If anything, Mrs. Tobin sounded like the bruiser. Could that be why she had discouraged Becky from snooping around?

The front door opened, and Mr. Tobin went

marching off into the woods. Becky stood stone still. She tried to melt into the siding of the house and blend seamlessly into the shadows. The light from the kitchen cast a square of yellow onto the grass a few feet away. But in a flash, it was snuffed out. Becky listened and was sure she heard the soft padding of feet throughout the house.

Sure that she was alone, Becky continued searching around the house. There were more strange bottles of some kind of liquid Becky didn't dare guess at. In addition to that, she saw strange and ugly statues, some no bigger than a walnut, others the size of an ear of corn. They had flat, dead-looking faces carved in big heads with spindly bodies contorted into gruesome poses. Something inside Becky told her not to touch them or get near them. It felt as if they were screaming at her without making a single sound.

Without any clear reason, Becky's heart began to pound. Other than the fact that she was trespassing on the Tobin property, there was no reason she should be panicking so. It was as if her body knew something was amiss, but her eyes had yet to lock in on it. She looked around but saw nothing in the moonlight.

The question that had been nagging Becky since

she first saw the Tobin house was, what did she expect to find? What did she think was going to materialize? She had no answer, and now that she was back where she'd started, at the front of the house, she had nothing to show for it except the strange smells and homely statues she'd have forever stamped in her memory.

So the Tobins were strange. Mr. Tobin probably started the fire at Mr. Ruthmeyer's. But there is no proof.

Becky was frustrated. Her gut had led her here. She couldn't go home empty-handed, even if she was the only one who knew she had paid the Tobins a visit.

When she was about to head back in the direction she had come, she saw a tiny light. She wouldn't have seen it when she'd first dashed to the house. It was a flickering lantern near a small shed. She was sure Mr. Tobin was deep inside the woods. The problem was that there was nowhere for her to hide until she reached it.

The light flickered, beckoning her. She looked to her left, to her right, her heart pounding in her chest, and after a big deep breath, she bolted toward the glimmer. Each stride made her feel exposed. The dim light from the half moon felt like a spotlight. She was sure a shotgun explosion was going to freeze her in her tracks. But there was nothing. Nothing but a horrible smell.

You numbskull, Becky, you snuck up on the outhouses, she thought.

But she quickly changed her mind when she saw the window. Outhouses didn't have windows. Who would ever think a window on their outhouse was a good thing or even proper? Becky knew she was a little wild at times, but even she felt that would have been a stone's throw from sinful.

So if this wasn't the outhouse, what was it? And why did it stink?

Carefully, Becky pressed her back against the wall. She had to breathe through her mouth in order to prevent herself from gagging. As much as she hated to admit it, some of the shanties she'd gone to with Martha and Teddy had also had peculiar odors. Becky knew some people lived much harder lives than she did. She knew what an outhouse smelled like. This was not an outhouse, and that smell was not from the natural movements of the human body. It was something worse. If Becky had had to describe it, she couldn't leave out the word "evil."

The sounds of the night were clear and sharp in her ears. Becky heard the crickets and a soft breeze that brought no relief from the smell that surrounded this structure. Part of her wanted to just go. She'd seen enough to know the Tobins were strange. She'd heard enough to see she had been wrong about who was the tough guy in the family. And her nose wanted to pull itself off her face and run away from the smell. But still, she had to look in the window.

Small plaques with symbols carved in them grabbed her attention as she looked over the shack. A thick padlock hung on the door, and more strange tiles that looked like angry children had made them adorned all sides of the structure.

"It's too dark. You probably won't even see anything," she muttered as she inched her way to the window. It was filthy, with streaks of grime on the inside and out. She cupped her hands over her eyes and squinted inside.

What she saw stopped her heart.

By the light of a single candle, she spied two mounds like fresh grave plots. A hand was protruding from one. It moved.

Becky clamped her hand over her mouth and ran back to the main house, where she slipped into a shadow and stayed there for what felt like hours. She wanted to dash back to the woods, but Mr. Tobin was in there. If she ran into him, her goose would be cooked.

As she tried to collect herself and muster up enough courage to run to the safety of the woods, she heard a scratching noise in the wall behind her as if something was trapped or scurrying between the insulation and the siding. It stopped and started. Becky remembered hearing the same thing in the pantry at home. A mouse had gotten stuck between the inside and outside walls. Either it had shinnied itself loose or the creature had died. Either way, the scratching had eventually stopped.

This scratching didn't stop, though, and it sounded as if something was trying to get through the wall to Becky. She didn't dare move as she waited for it to pass. What was she afraid of? It was just an animal scurrying inside the wall. It wasn't like those two mounds of dirt inside the shed just a few yards away. Becky suddenly became very cold.

A window opened high above her. She could hear a female voice singing softly, like a mother might sing a lullaby. But the tone of the woman's voice didn't sound soothing. It was raspy, and the words sounded jumbled and incoherent. Becky looked up.

Leaning almost completely out the window was the woman with the purple scarf around her head.

Like she had been at the cemetery, she was suspended at an unnatural angle, and her head was slowly scanning back and forth as if she was looking for something.

She's not looking for something. She's looking for you, *Rebecca.*

Becky didn't move. She didn't breathe. She didn't blink. She stared at the grotesque, unnatural thing that was surveying the land like a dog might patrol its property.

Just then, from the woods came Mr. Tobin. He lumbered back to the house, stomped up the porch steps, and slammed the door behind him. The woman withdrew into the house as if someone had yanked her backward. But there was no shouting, no yelling. It was silent like a tomb. Becky realized that the sounds of nature had stopped. She remembered what she had seen when this same blanket of muteness had settled over the Old Brick Cemetery. She didn't want to see any more.

Pulling strength up from the very bottoms of her feet, Becky tore off for the woods. She was afraid her footsteps were even louder than they had been in the bone yard. It was as if she was running across glass, shattering it with each step. But it was just leaves and brush. She was thankful she'd worn her pants, as they were tugged and yanked in all directions by the sticker bushes she was plowing through. Her heart was pounding in her ears, and she panted like a wild animal, gulping air into her burning lungs. She didn't stop. She couldn't. Something would pop up behind her and drag her back to the Tobin place, and no one would ever hear from her again.

She kept running until she got to the remains of Mr. Ruthmeyer's home. Just a few steps and she'd be on her daddy's property. That was home.

She stopped and tried to catch her breath and listen. If anything was behind her, she couldn't see it or hear it. With one last gulp of air, she ran to the safety of the tobacco field.

It was as if a door had shut behind her as soon as she touched the property. A feeling of relief and security swept over her, and she stopped to regain her composure. Her hair was a sweaty mess beneath her hat. When she tried to tuck her blouse back inside her trousers, she felt that they were both covered with burrs.

"What in the world was all that?" Becky mused, confident she was safe as she made her way back home. It felt as if she'd been gone for hours. Any minute, the sky would start to lighten, and the new day would begin.

But as she hurried toward her house, she heard a car pulling down the road. She peeked through the leaves and was sure it was Teddy's auto. Was Fanny in the car? Was Martha? Were they dropping Fanny off or looking for Becky?

Suddenly Becky had the image of her mother stopping in her room to check on her, only to see she'd shinnied down the trellis again. There was no describing the trouble she'd be in. Forgetting the Tobins for the moment, Becky began to jog home. But when she got there, nothing was like she'd imagined.

CHAPTER ELEVEN

The house was quiet. The porch lights were on. Everything looked normal. Had Kitty been tipped off that Becky wasn't home, there would be a faint light in her drawing room, where she'd be waiting up. But everything was dark.

Becky shinnied up the trellis and quietly slipped into her room. She snapped on the delicate lamp on her desk and let out a long, tired sigh. Before she could let herself relax, she pulled off her hat and pants and inspected the burrs stuck to everything. It would be an impossible project to pull each one out of the fabric.

"I'll worry about that tomorrow," she muttered. Without making a sound, she opened her bedroom door and walked down the hallway. The clock on the table at the edge of the stairs read ten minutes to one.

"That can't be. It felt like I was gone for hours," Becky whispered.

Doubting the time on this clock, she went downstairs to look at the grandfather clock that had been right as rain for as long as she could remember. When she looked at it, she was even more frustrated. It said *nine* to one.

"Ugh." She shrugged and went back to her room.

The last few hours, whether it had been two or ten, swirled around in her head, mixing into a soup of more mystery and questions than she'd had when she first snuck out of her house. Inside her fortress, Becky picked up her sketchbook and quickly jotted down the images she had seen that evening. The remains of the Ruthmeyer house, the Tobin homestead, the strange statues and plaques on and around the house, and the horrifying mounds of dirt inside that lonely shack were all transferred onto Becky's pages.

When she drew the woman with the purple head scarf, she felt a shiver run over her. How had she been able to hang out the window without falling?

Becky swallowed and shut the book. She yawned, stretched her arms over her head, and climbed into bed. Normally, she'd leave the window open and let the cool breeze float over her while she snuggled beneath the warmth of her blankets. But tonight, she shut the window and slipped the lock into place. After switching off the light, she stood in the darkness for a moment, letting her eyes adjust. She looked out the window. Nothing moved. There wasn't even a breeze. But Becky got the feeling there was something out there, hiding in the shadows like she had been.

That was when she saw the tiny flicker of light out at the cemetery. Someone was out there again. Becky didn't dare go investigate. They'd get a clean sneak tonight. Becky told herself she was all in, and that was why she wasn't going to investigate.

The truth was she was getting the heebie-jeebies, and no droppers were going to get the goods on her in her own backyard. Nope. She was staying put.

Becky thought of the little girl who had been crying when she first saw the men with their mouths sewn closed. She had said that they were stealing the dirt and disturbing the old folks. Tomorrow, Becky would go to the cemetery when the sun was high and bright in the sky and nothing could be hiding in the shadows.

When she woke up the following morning, she felt as if she was barely running on two cylinders. Her legs ached, and when she looked at all the dirt and debris she'd tracked into her room, she gasped. Her clothes were covered in burrs that pricked Becky's fingers as she tried to remove them.

"Rats," she said.

"Miss Becky?" Moxley asked through the door. "Your mama be waitin' for you in the dining room."

"Thanks, Moxley," Becky replied. "What time is it?"

"Almost ten."

Becky's eyes bugged, and she gasped. Almost ten? What was happening?

Within five minutes, she had scrubbed her face, gargled with Listerine until she spat out the burning liquid, brushed her hair, and dressed in one of her mother's favorite dresses. Yes, it was a pitiful attempt at gaining favor with her after having a blah attitude over yesterday's lunch and then sleeping in like a hobo at a bus station. She dashed down the stairs, nearly colliding with Fanny.

"Who would have thought that a day of civilized

shopping and not cavorting through a graveyard would wear you out?" Fanny asked with a smile.

"Yeah, I guess that was it. Did you go out last night?" Becky asked, remembering the car she had heard just as she was coming from the Tobin farm.

"Well, yes. It was great fun." She smoothed the front of her new dress, which was such a bright yellow she could be spotted from a mile away.

"Becky?" Kitty called.

"Excuse me, Fanny. Mama's calling." Becky shuffled past her cousin and found her mother sitting at the dining room table with a cup of coffee in front of her.

"Hi, Mama. I don't know what came over me. I was plumb tuckered out."

Becky strolled up to Kitty and kissed her playfully on the head before taking her seat.

Moxley brought her a cup of coffee, and she declined any food. She didn't want to be a burden and force Lucretia to cook something special when she'd obviously missed breakfast.

"Becky, do you know a man by the name of Adam White?" Kitty asked with a sly look on her face.

Becky nearly spit up her coffee.

"Um, well, yes, uhm. I think I do. I'd probably

recognize his face. Why?" Becky's heart was pounding in her chest.

"He came calling this morning," Kitty said.

"He what?" Becky barked. "Why would he do that?"

"He's a Yankee," Kitty said, pinching her lips together.

"Yes. I think I remember him being a Yankee," Becky stuttered. "But there are quite a few Yankees around, and they're fine gents."

"I don't know how I feel about you cavorting around with a Yankee. Here I've been introducing you to the finest Southern thoroughbreds, and you insist on turning your nose up at them." Kitty cleared her throat. "I'm going to talk with your father about it."

"Talk to him about what?" Becky just knew this was going to end badly, but she couldn't help the words that were forming in her mouth. If she could just hold them back a little longer.

"I'm going to talk to him about this Adam White fellow, who thinks he can arrive on our doorstep unannounced and ask to speak with my one and only child." Kitty took a calm sip of coffee, her eyes never leaving her daughter's.

"And when do you plan on talking to me about this?"

"I'm talking to you right now, Becky. Fanny has said that you've painted the town with this man and that he's also made advances to her." Kitty blinked. "You might think I'm doing this to be cruel, but I'm looking out for your well-being and trying to protect your reputation."

"Mama, I am twenty-two years old. I can make my own decisions about who I cavort with. Mr. White is a hardworking man with a good family that just happens to be from the North," Becky stated.

"You've met his family?" Kitty's right eyebrow shot up as she asked this question.

"No. But he's told me all about them. He works as a pressman. It's a respectable profession, Mama, and he's…"

"And he's flirting with your cousin Fanny when you aren't available. That does not sound respectable to me. Now when I talk to your father…"

"You can't tell me that you are actually taking Fanny's word about this? Mama, you see how she acts whenever you invite anyone over to the house." Becky was trying to stay calm. It was as if she was surrounded by swarming bees but knew if she swatted, they'd sting her. She was helpless.

"Rebecca, you are my daughter, and I think you are beautiful and intelligent. It isn't my fault that Fanny has the kind of confidence I wish you had. You spend so much time in that cemetery. And don't mistake me, I love Teddy and Martha. But Fanny is a completely different person since she went off to Paris. She was exposed to culture and cuisine and different kinds of people. It made her a very interesting person." Kitty smiled, but Becky wasn't buying.

"It made her a snob. Not that she was ever pleasant to begin with," Becky replied. "So did you shoo Mr. White away for good, or will he be back?"

Kitty cleared her throat. "I'm sure I don't know. I told him you were unavailable and that he should send word he's calling next time."

Becky could have pointed out her mother's hypocrisy if she were looking for a long fight. She could have dragged it out for hours, if not days, reminding her mother that meeting new people meant meeting Northerners, too. And in Savannah, if a girl knew too many strangers, well, there was a name that might be associated with that sort of reputation. But she pinched her lips together.

"Where is Daddy? Can we have this talk with him now?" Becky asked.

"He's out in the fields and can't be bothered. We'll discuss it tonight. Your father and I will discuss this tonight."

"Are you sure you don't want Fanny there, too? I'm sure she's had some experience in Paris that will help you decide my life for me," Becky added before standing from the table.

"I don't think I like your tone, young lady."

"It seems to me that you don't like much about me, Mama. But thank goodness Fanny is here. At least she can keep up appearances."

Becky stormed out of the dining room and once again caught Fanny lingering just outside the door as if she were preoccupied with some discoloration in the wallpaper.

Becky huffed and stormed outside without saying another word. She headed toward the cemetery for spite if nothing else. As she walked, her mind was a jumble of quips she wished she'd said. She loved her mother, but this was getting to be too much. Kitty didn't like the idea of her daughter being unwed at such an old age. But worse, she didn't like that her daughter wasn't interested in the busters Kitty was introducing her to. Fanny fawned all over anyone that came to the house even though Becky knew she wouldn't give any one of them the time of day if she ran into them on the street.

Before she realized it, she'd walked to the far end of the cemetery, where the old entrance still stood. And just outside that entrance, she saw a flivver that looked familiar.

"I was hoping if I waited, I might catch you," Adam shouted from the front seat of his car.

Everything Becky had been thinking melted away as she looked at his clean-shaven face and neatly combed hair.

"You look like the cat's pajamas. You get all dolled up for Fanny?" Becky asked, only half kidding.

"Don't move," Adam said as he shut off his car and hopped out. He was dressed in neat slacks with suspenders and a starched, clean shirt.

Becky thought he had stepped right out of a postcard. She stood still and waited as he approached. He stood right in front of her, looking down his strong, broad chest and smirking.

"No, I didn't get dolled up to see Fanny. I got dolled up to see your mother." He chuckled. "But I think she heard my accent and made her decision."

Becky took a deep breath and slowly nodded.

"Did I get you in trouble?"

"You know me, Adam. A day without trouble is

like a day without sunshine," Becky chirped, putting her hands on her hips.

"Trouble is your middle name. And I don't like spending a day without trouble in it either. What's the big idea leaving me at Willie's?" He took her right hand in his big paw.

"I'm sorry about that. I was just so frustrated. Fanny's got everyone wrapped around her little finger, and when you…"

"When I what?" He folded his arms across his chest.

Becky could have swooned. Adam had to know how handsome he was and that he was using it to weaken her knees.

"When you let her manipulate you the way she does everyone else, it makes me…"

Becky gasped when Adam took hold of her by the shoulders. It wasn't violent or scary. Quite the opposite. He stooped down and looked into her eyes.

"Rebecca Madeline Mackenzie, the only woman who has ever or will ever have me wrapped around their finger is you." He leaned even closer to her. "Tell me you believe me."

"I…believe you," she said, her voice just over a whisper.

"That doesn't sound like you do." He let his lips brush against her skin.

"I do, Adam. I believe you."

"Good. Now kiss me."

Becky smiled, wrapped her arms around Adam's thick neck, and pulled him to her. Now she was sure time stood still. Under the dilapidated entrance of the Old Brick Cemetery, Adam and Becky kissed, making it the most romantic place on Earth.

After a few moments of kisses slipped in between apologies and even a few wisecracks, Adam took Becky's hand and began to stroll with her farther into the bone yard.

"What is it you like about this place?" Adam asked.

"It's peaceful. And the spirits are friendly." She winked at Adam. "They accept me, and I am very grateful for that. It's a shame the people alive in my house can't be the same way."

The moss hanging from the trees provided not only cool shade but privacy that Becky and Adam rarely found anyplace else. They kissed a bit more, and Becky had all but forgotten about her adventure the night before until they came to a sight that made Becky almost cry.

"What happened here?" Adam said, pointing to a hole in the dirt.

"Oh no. It looks like someone has tampered with this grave," Becky replied. "This is where...*they* were."

"Who?" Adam asked.

Becky explained what had happened the night they'd had their fight. That she'd cut through the cemetery and found people here. She left out no details.

"Sewn shut? Their mouths were sewn shut. Are you sure?"

"Yes, and then last night, I..." Becky wanted to tell Adam about her discoveries of the previous night. But she was suddenly overwhelmed by voices crying and yelling and begging for her help. She was sure she heard that little girl who had been crying the night she saw the men with their mouths sewn shut and the woman with the purple head scarf.

"Beck. Are you okay?"

"Do you hear them? Do you hear them crying?" She took hold of his arm to steady herself.

"I don't hear anything but us. What is it?"

"They're all talking at once. I can't understand what they are saying, but it has something to do with this." She pointed to the disturbed graves. "They're using the soil. The ground that these people are buried in is blessed, and they are using it for something...unholy."

"How do you know this? What are you talking about?" Adam looked very worried as he held Becky in his arms.

"Take me to your car. Quick," Becky said as light-headedness washed over her and her legs gave out.

Before she could hit the ground, Adam slipped his arms around her and lifted her up. Holding her close to him, he took her out of the cemetery and placed her gingerly in the passenger's seat.

CHAPTER TWELVE

"*B*ecky. Sweetheart," Adam whispered. "Here. Lift your head. Take a sip."

Becky felt the cool metal neck of Adam's flask against her lips. She let him pour the whiskey, and she swallowed quickly. The rush of burning bourbon made her cough, and she was glad for it.

"That's my girl," he said. "Come on. Open your eyes."

Becky did as she was told, and her eyes fluttered open.

"What in the world happened? We were just bumping gums, and then everything just tipped over. I feel like a flat tire."

"You scared me," Adam admitted.

His eyes were wide, and even though Becky

wanted to set his mind at ease, she couldn't help but enjoy the feeling of being in his arms and hearing his heart pounding through his shirt.

"I'm all right now." She scooted up in the passenger's seat and looked into the cemetery entrance. "We've got a problem. But I don't know what to do about it."

"Me neither. But if going into that place is like a dry gulch to you, then sweetheart, I want you to stay away. At least don't go in by yourself."

"I'm usually never by myself," she muttered. "But lately there hasn't been anyone to come see me."

She didn't think Adam knew what she really meant—that the spirits she'd grown to know and care for were not paying her any visits. It was as if they were hiding or worse, being prevented from coming out. They were prisoners in their graves. The thought of that broke Becky's heart.

"Promise me you won't go in by yourself. Take Fanny or…"

"Fanny? You're off your rocker. I wouldn't take her temperature let alone take her into this place," Becky snapped, quickly regaining her composure.

"Yikes, gal, forget I asked. Just promise me you won't go by yourself."

When Adam looked at her with his deep blue eyes, she let out a little sigh. "I promise."

"Good, now let's get you home." He leaned back in the driver's seat, started the engine, and started to pull away.

"Better drop me a good ways from the front of the house. The last thing you need is Kitty or Fanny catching a glimpse of you dropping me off. They'll run to Daddy and have all sorts of tall tales to report to him."

"Do you think your father is a reasonable man?" Adam asked as he whipped around the dirt road.

"He's the most. My daddy knows more than any man I've ever met. And you know he doesn't have anything more than a second-grade education. Yet look at all this. I swear he's got tobacco in his veins."

"I look forward to meeting him." Adam smirked as he hit the gas, making Becky squeal and laugh.

He finally dropped her off behind a patch of trees so she could sneak back to the house without anyone taking notice. But not before kissing her again. It was hard for her to pull away from him, but with one last kiss and the promise to see him soon, Becky dashed off toward the house.

Just as she was about to start her ascent of the

trellis to her room, a familiar voice came from the bushes.

"Becky and Adam sitting in a tree. K-I-S-S-I-N-G," Teddy said, tipping his straw hat down over his eyes as he sauntered over.

"What are you doing here?" Becky asked.

"I've come to rescue you." He jerked his thumb toward the house. "After spending the evening with Martha and your cousin, I'm all in." He rolled his eyes.

"So that was you I heard driving away early this morning. I was sure I recognized the sound of that old flivver." Becky winked. "But I was too far inside the tobacco field to flag you down, or else I would have."

"In the tobacco field?"

"It's a long story." Becky shook her head and patted her finger waves into place much like her mother did when she was worried about something.

"I got the time. What you say we blow this pop stand and go pick up Martha?"

"I say let's make tracks before someone sees us." Becky felt a twinge of guilt at leaving the house without saying good-bye to her mother or giving her the slightest hint as to where she was going or with whom. But after their "conversation," Becky didn't feel it was worth telling her mother where she was going. She'd disapprove no matter what, and she'd have Fanny to reassure her of Becky's bad decision-making.

Once they passed the sign that read Welcome to Poole County, Becky let out a sigh of relief. It was as if there was something hanging over not just the Mackenzie plantation but the whole area, and Becky was finally free of it. She knew it was all in her head. The fight with Kitty was the primary culprit.

Seeing the Bourdeaux estate and Martha sitting on the porch with a tray of mint juleps at her elbow was enough to make Becky forget all her troubles.

"Quite frankly, Becky, I don't know how you tolerate that cousin of yours," Martha said as she sipped her cool, minty bourbon. "I certainly didn't mind that she wanted to tag along, but what a drag."

"Is it true that Adam's carrying a torch for her?" Becky knew if anyone would tell her the truth, it was Martha. And she braced for it to hurt. Even though Adam had said he wasn't interested in Fanny, Becky wasn't a hundred percent sold.

"What? Who told you that? Let me guess: Fanny." Martha rolled her eyes.

"She said he took her around the floor and that her feet barely touched the ground because he was holding her so close," Becky said after taking a sip of her own mint julep.

"Ha! Her feet didn't touch the ground because she was smashing the poor palooka's toes with every step. Becky, I'm saying this as your best friend. She might be put together like a sheba, but she doesn't hold a candle to you when it comes to cutting the rug. And most guys want more than just a dame on their arm."

"Says who?" Teddy interrupted with his eyes closed. He was sitting on the porch steps next to the swing with his back against the porch railing.

"No one is talking to you, Mr. Rockdale," Martha quipped.

"Look, Becky, you know I love you, darling. But as distasteful as you find your cousin, she certainly knows how to run in the races. In fact, I'd put my money on that filly any day." Teddy chuckled.

"Don't listen to him. He's not running on all cylinders." Martha poked him with the toe of her shoe. "Fanny is just a tomato, and anyone who spends more than five minutes with her can figure that out."

"I'm just being honest." Teddy reached up to tickle Martha behind her knee, making her squirm and swat at him.

"I don't begrudge the woman her looks. But when she's talking out of turn to Mama, well, that just tans my hide." Becky finally flipped her hair behind her and took a sip of her drink. "I don't want to talk about her any more. She gives me indigestion."

"Martha, dear?" Teddy stood from the porch steps and bowed deeply.

"Yes, Theodore, sweetheart?" Martha replied.

"Does your mother have any more of this sweetened noodle juice inside?" he asked with a sly grin.

"Of course. It's like the Sahara Desert out here today." Martha fanned herself. "Would you mind refreshing our glasses, too? You are so dapper."

"For you ladies, I'd lasso the moon," he replied. "Try not to miss me while I'm away."

"It's not you I'll be missing but the mint julep," Becky teased.

After a deep laugh, Teddy disappeared inside the house. Becky scooted closer to Martha on the swing and began to tell her about what she had seen at the Tobin place.

Martha gasped. "Becky! Now I don't think you are running on all cylinders."

"Keep your voice down. I don't want Teddy spilling the beans to Kitty and Judge." Becky put her hand on Martha's. "Look, I need you to come with me."

"Come with you where?"

"Back to the Tobin place," Becky whispered.

"Back? Why in the world would you want to go back?" Martha grimaced.

"Mr. Tobin went to check on something in the woods. I want to know what it is."

Becky was sure it had something to do with the men whose lips were sewn shut or the buried stiffs in the shed that turned out to be not so stiff.

"Becky, sometimes the mysteries of life are better left as mysteries," Martha replied and squeezed her friend's hand. "And that woman they have in their employ? I've seen her around town. I don't know a soul who has ever spoken with her. Even when she accompanies Mrs. Tobin, I don't see them speak. But there is something odd about that woman."

"She was in my graveyard," Becky said. Martha had no words and looked into Becky's eyes. "She was in *my* graveyard…digging."

It was as if an unspoken rule had been broken.

Martha, like Teddy, knew of Becky's feelings toward the Old Brick Cemetery and those buried in it. The idea that an interloper had decided to plant stakes in the sacred place that Becky had named herself protector of, well, it was an affront. From the look on Becky's face, it was even more than that. It was a shot across the bow.

"I was sure Mr. Tobin was heavy-handed with Mrs. Tobin. That would explain why she fled to the arms of Mr. Ruthmeyer, if she indeed did do that," Becky said. "But when I heard their conversation, I had to pick my jaw up off the ground. Sure enough, he was browbeaten by the lady of the house. So I want to know what he's got going on in the woods where he seeks solace."

"You're probably going to be sorely disappointed. I'll bet my new silk stockings he's built himself a shack back there and has it stocked with bathtub gin and girlie pictures." Martha chuckled.

"I hope you are right. So you'll come with me?" Becky asked.

"You know I can't let you have all the fun." Martha leaned into her friend, and they touched foreheads.

"Break it up," Teddy said, returning with their drinks.

The rest of the afternoon was pleasant. The trio picked up Fanny that evening and went out to Willie's speakeasy. Becky and Martha had agreed to go snooping the following day while the sun was up. But it turned out the sun provided very little comfort or cover.

CHAPTER THIRTEEN

*B*ecky took a deep breath as she waited on the front porch for Martha to arrive. Over and over in her head, she went over the path they would take, where they would leave the car, how far they'd have to travel on foot, and what to do if they were discovered. That last part Becky put out of her mind quickly. Thinking of the worst-case scenario often led to that thing happening, so she pushed it aside.

Oh, you know that Martha is probably right. Mr. Tobin probably has an old shack out there with heaven knows what kind of junk in it. It'll be a big bust.

Still, her own words didn't bring her any comfort.

She peeked in the front door and squinted at

the grandfather clock. If Martha didn't hurry, Fanny would be up from her morning nap, and Kitty would insist they drag her with. The whole plan would have to be scrapped for another day, and something inside Becky made her feel there wasn't much time left. She didn't know why she had that feeling, but it was there, and it was relentless.

"Finally," Becky sighed as she saw the dust kicking up at the end of the long drive. She scooped up the large picnic basket that had a few snacks from Lucretia tucked inside and also a change of clothes. There was no way she was going to ruin another outfit and have to explain it to her mother.

"Where are you off to in such a hurry?" Fanny said through a long yawn.

Becky's body slumped right after she froze in her tracks. "Martha asked me to run a couple errands with her."

"Did you tell Aunt Kitty where you were off to?" Fanny asked, looking down her nose at Becky as if she were wearing a crown.

"My mother doesn't need to be bothered every time I blow my nose," Becky replied. "I'll be back in an hour, two tops."

"I'll run and tell her you're leaving," Fanny said as

if those words would somehow get Becky to change her mind and stay put.

"I'm sure you will," Becky muttered before marching in Martha's direction to meet her halfway down the driveway. As soon as she hopped into the car, Martha turned the wheels, pulled forward, backed up, ground the gears, and stepped on the clutch, making the jalopy jerk and stop before finally getting the machine to lurch forward and keep going.

"Are you going to be in trouble?" Martha asked.

"Seems like I always am. Why should today be any different?" Becky smiled and pointed down the dirt road in the direction of the burnt remains of the Ruthmeyer farm.

They chatted normally for the first mile or two, but by the time they parked the car in a patch of bald cypress that had grown wild and provided an almost impenetrable cover, they realized how nervous they were.

"I can't believe we are doing this," Martha whispered.

"What else would you be doing today?" Becky grumped. "We go into shantytowns and down dark alleys for a joint with dancing. This is a slice of peach pie compared to that. And we do all that in heels. Here." Becky handed Martha a pair of flat shoes with cleats on the bottom that she'd swiped from her basement.

"What am I supposed to do with these?" Martha chuckled.

"Eat them. What do you think? Put them on. They were my father's when he tried to play golf. Turns out Daddy doesn't have the patience to swing a stick at a one-inch ball to knock it into a hole a mile away," Becky joked.

"Who would have thought that?" Martha laughed. "Your father trying to golf is like a gator trying not to have teeth."

"Okay. Now, put this on." Becky handed Martha a hat.

"Are you crazy? I just had my hair done."

"Martha Bourdeaux, if you don't put this hat on, you are going to get burrs in your hair, and they will have to shave your head bald. Now take this." Becky thrust the hat at her again.

"Oh, if I have to, let me wear the Panama. I look just dreadful in a poor boy." She wiggled her fingers at the tan Panama hat Becky had in her left hand and waved away the slouchy, baggy poor-boy hat Becky had in her right hand.

"You are too much," Becky said, quickly slapping

the poor boy on her own head and stuffing her red locks deep inside.

"See, now, you look like the bee's knees in that. I'd look like Tugboat Annie." Martha stuffed her hair up in the Panama hat, cuffed her pants, and polished the tops of her golf shoes on the backs of her trousers. "I'm ready."

"You look adorable. Considering we are playing at private detecting, we look swell. I like these trousers. They give you room to move."

Martha wiggled her hips.

"Well, you are the cat's pajamas. I think Teddy would be impressed. Okay, let's cheese it and get moving."

Becky and Martha quietly and carefully slipped into the woods, heading in the direction of the Tobin place. It was cool in the shade of the trees. Their loose clothes managed to keep any bloodsucking insects off their skin. Squirrels and birds skittered through the grass and leaves at an almost constant pace that helped to muffle their footsteps.

All of a sudden, the forest grew darker. A low ceiling of clouds appeared and blanketed the whole sky. Martha sniffed the air.

"That's funny. It hasn't smelled like rain all day.

Now, all of a sudden, it smells like we're going to need to build an ark," she whispered.

"Look there." Becky pointed. It was the Tobin house, perched on that hill and looking down at them as if it had eyes in the windows.

Martha shimmied. "It gives me the heebie-jeebies. I'm starting to think this was a bad idea."

"We won't go anywhere near the house," Becky said. "Mr. Tobin took off from the porch and ran into the woods there. Let's get behind whatever he's got planted in there and see what we can see."

Martha nodded and followed Becky deeper into the woods. Along the way, they both started to notice thick sticks with orange paint sticking out of the ground at what looked like random intervals. Just as Martha was about to say something, they both froze. Voices. Male voices. The women crouched and listened.

"I'll have more in about two weeks," one voice said.

"Earl, I really could use some of that now. I know you got plenty in the still, and I know you are goin' to sell it. Why not to me? My money is just as good as anyone else's."

"Well, that's where you're wrong, Mr. Gavin. You see, I know my wife had been down to your shop, and you didn't barely accommodate her. Now, as I see it, that ain't the way a man does business. So now you'll see how it feels to be high-hatted."

"But Earl, that was just a misunderstanding. I didn't know your wife had felt that way. I... thought...she was..."

"You thought the same as the rest of the people in this town. That she has a bad reputation on account of that Ruthmeyer. You thought she was loose. We'll see what the town folk say when they see R.H. Gavin himself greet my wife at the door of his very own general store."

"I could report you. The coppers would love to know where this still is. They'd have you behind bars in violation of the Volstead Act faster than you could slap a tick," Gavin said with a shaky voice.

"You threatening me?"

Suddenly there was movement farther back in the trees. Becky and Martha took hold of each other's hands and stayed perfectly still. Through the brush, they could see the trousers of the men talking. Becky peeked her head up slightly. She saw a dirty gray metal container balancing on a bed of bricks. A coiled dirty black tube ran from the container to a barrel that was connected to another barrel by a copper tube about four inches around. A fire smoldered under the metal container. Black soot covered its bottom.

As Becky strained her eyes, she finally saw the jugs and jars around the still. There were also the creepy statues and plaques and carvings strewn all around like miniature guards and lookouts.

From far behind, two more men emerged from the woods. One man was wearing tattered pants and boots with holes in the bottoms. The other man was familiar. Just then fear seized Becky's heart.

It was the man from the Crazy Calico, the one she had danced with. He turned in their direction just as Becky pulled her head down out of view.

"If you're threatening me, Mr. Gavin, then I'm going to leave you here to talk to these fellows. And then I'll send Leelee down. If you'll excuse me," Mr. Tobin hissed.

"No. Wait! Tobin. You've got it all wrong! I'm not threatening anyone! Tobin! Fellas! You don't need to get Leelee. Trust me. I'll just wait. I'll go about my business, and you tell Mrs. Tobin to come by my store and…"

"We don't deliver messages," the man Becky had danced with hissed.

"But this is a mistake. I don't need to see Leelee. I don't. Please. Fellas, look. Let me go. I won't say anything to anyone. You have my word as a gentle-man," Gavin blubbered.

"You see any gentlemen around these parts, Edward?" the man in the torn trousers and holey boots asked.

"Not a one, Zeke," replied the man Becky had danced with. It was no wonder he had gotten sore when Becky had mentioned the Ruthmeyer fire. If Zeke was muscle for Mr. Tobin, he wouldn't tolerate anyone flapping their gums about his bread and butter.

"Becky. Becky, we need to get out of here. I don't want to be a witness to no murder. I've seen enough. So Tobin has a moonshine still back here. Ain't no different from what I said before. And I'll bet under one of those jugs is a stash of nudie pictures. Now let's call it a day," Martha hissed.

"We can't leave. They'll see us for sure. Close your eyes and don't move until I tell you," Becky whispered back and turned back to the scene unfolding.

Before Martha could protest, everything in the forest went quiet. Becky felt her heart starting to race and pound like cymbals in her ears. She put her index finger slowly to her lips, to which Martha nodded. Just then, the woman with the scarf on her head appeared.

"Leelee, I didn't mean anything," Mr. Gavin blubbered. "I'd never turn you in. You know that. I just lost my head. I've been a faithful customer for years. You can always trust me."

"Shh, Mr. Gavin. It's too late for talk." Leelee's voice clutched Becky's heart like a vise. It was the voice she had heard from the window. That hadn't been Mrs. Tobin being bossy at all. It was this waif-like maid they called Leelee.

"No. Leelee. Whatever you're thinking of doing, don't do it. I have a family. I have a store to run," Gavin stammered.

"You'll be able to run your business. But not much else."

Becky lifted her head and squinted through the leaves. She saw Leelee pick up one of the little jars that had been placed around the still. It was filled with dirt and something else Becky didn't dare guess at. But it wasn't seeing that jar that broke her heart. There was something else.

"Mr. Wilcox?" Becky gasped.

Standing off to the side, unseen by anyone else, was the spirit of her favorite friend from the Old Brick Cemetery. His face looked worn, and his eyes darted around as if he had no idea where he was. And they were filled with tears. The dirt Leelee was using for her spell or magic or whatever it was must be from Mr. Wilcox's grave.

Becky watched helplessly as he silently cried out in frustration and what Becky could only guess was anger. He had lived the life of a hardworking man, not unlike Becky's own father. He was supposed to be waiting peacefully to be escorted by St. Michael and the Lord's army of angels into paradise. Instead, he was being dragged unwillingly to this den so Leelee could use his burial ground for her own twisted purposes.

This wasn't just bootlegging. This was something much darker.

CHAPTER FOURTEEN

"*B*ecky?" Martha whispered.

Becky heard but didn't look at her friend.

Leelee took that jar of sacred dirt and other things and began to wave it around Gavin. He clenched his teeth and jerked like he was going to try and run away. But the two men, Zeke and Edward, took hold of his arms and held him fast. He begged Leelee not to put a curse on him. He promised her everything he had if she'd show mercy.

When Becky looked at the woman with the scarf wrapped so tightly around her head, she didn't see that same waif she had seen the day of the fire. *That* woman had looked like she might be helpful, like she might offer a firm but kind word of comfort to the distraught Mrs. Tobin. But this woman looked like a cat enjoying the slow death it was inflicting on a mouse.

"Don't cry, Mr. Gavin. You'll be all right." She smiled a wide, crooked grin as she shook the jar and stuck her fingers deep into the grit then smeared it on Gavin's shirt. He writhed and tried to pull away, but it was no use. "You go on home to your wife, and you go to work tomorrow. You'll see. You'll be fine… until you are not."

Zeke and Edward turned him loose only to laugh as Gavin tore himself away and began to stumble and blubber his way out of the woods and in the direction of the house.

"Becky?"

"Martha, we're in deep. I don't even know what I just saw, but I know we're in big trouble," Becky whispered while keeping her eyes on the group.

"Becky?"

Finally, Becky turned to Martha and saw that her friend's rosy complexion had turned white. She followed her gaze behind them to see two other men standing in the shadows of the trees, almost completely camouflaged. Their mouths were sewn shut. Their skin, once smooth and dark with life, was now ashy, with dirt and grime clinging to it. Their shoulders slumped with the weight of a version of life that shouldn't have been there. They were alive, but they weren't living things. They moved, but they saw nothing with their eyes, which looked like those of a boiled trout.

"Don't move." Becky's lips barely moved.

She and Martha were directly in the middle between the poor creatures dragged up from the graves in the shed and the hillbillies from the Crazy Calico. And it couldn't be overlooked that Leelee was still standing there, surveying the land.

Becky looked around the ground, moving just her eyes to see if there was anything they could use as weapons. The pickings were slim.

"Miss Leelee, what you call them here for?" Edward asked, pointing to the two things that were just a few yards from Becky and Martha. "You know I don't like them."

Leelee started to laugh out loud. She shook her head before setting down the jar of dirt that she'd smeared on Gavin. She picked up two mason jars of clear liquid and handed one to Edward and the other to Zeke. Both men were quick to take a sip.

"You don't like my pets. Better than blood-hounds, they are," Leelee cackled.

Becky and Martha looked at each other.

At that very second, Leelee stopped laughing and looked in their direction. She sneered, clapped her hands, and said something that Becky thought might have been French, but she couldn't be sure. Where was Fanny when she needed her?

With jerky, lumbering movements, the poor souls turned in Becky and Martha's direction and advanced. Without thinking, Becky grabbed Martha's hand. They jumped up and began to run.

"Get them! Don't let those boys escape!" Edward yelled.

But it wasn't from Edward that the poor souls took their direction. It was from the shriveled woman with the scarf around her head. Leelee was their master.

Becky didn't dare turn around to see what was happening behind her. Instead, she held Martha's hand tightly and felt as if she was doing nothing more than pulling a kite behind her.

Martha was quick on her feet until…

"Ooooph!" Martha's hand tore from Becky's.

When Becky turned around, she saw her friend

lying on the ground, stunned. The culprit that had tripped her up was an exposed tree root.

"Are you all right?" Becky asked.

"Yes. What were those things? What did we just see?" Martha panted.

"I don't know. But we need to…"

Just then, one of the poor souls burst through the brush and grabbed hold of Martha's leg. She screamed as Becky took hold of her arms and tugged. Martha kicked and squirmed and finally remembered the cleats on the bottoms of her shoes. Without a second's hesitation, she thrust her heel into the creature's blind eyes. It bellowed and let go of her.

"Come on!"

Becky hoisted her to her feet, and they continued running. The other poor soul was quickly approaching but stumbled over his partner, who had fallen to the ground, still holding his face.

The women made it to Martha's car, where Becky dove into the driver's seat as Martha jumped into the back seat and ducked. Within seconds, the engine roared, and they were on the dirt road.

"Where are you going? Your house is that way." Martha pointed behind them.

"Quick. We need to change back into our dresses," Becky said as she pulled off her cap and tore the shirt off her back.

"Oh, if your cousin Fanny saw what we were doing." Martha chuckled nervously. "I do believe Miss Kitty would have you sent away to a convent."

The car swerved all over the road as Becky undressed down to her intimates before slipping her dress over her head, her foot on the gas the entire time. There were gasps and grunts and a couple of screams as she nearly drove them into the ditch, into an oncoming truck loaded with hay, and over a raccoon lazily crossing the road. Finally, they looked as respectable as two women who had just run through the woods could and pulled the car up in front of a small farm stand and general store.

"I didn't know this little place was here," Martha said.

"Me either. But I could use a cold drink," Becky said as she patted her hair into place and adjusted her garter belts before getting out of the car.

"Becky, if my father knew you had been driving my car, he would have himself one grand tantrum," Martha chuckled. "Everyone for eight counties knows all about why you don't have a car. It's common knowledge, and I think that whole incident has gone down as a feat that cannot be duplicated. Sort of like a circus act that…"

"I don't think this is the time or place to discuss my driving record," Becky snapped as she got out of the car and slammed the door. "And if you'll take a look…not a scratch on her."

"That's a miracle." Martha climbed out of the back seat, adjusting her bra strap and smoothing out her dress. No one inside the store or milling around outside paid too much attention to the new customers.

"I think we made a clean break," Becky said quietly.

"Becky, what was all that? I've seen moonshiners before. There's an old man with a wagon that goes door to door at my Uncle Samburg's shanty in Kentucky. He's as pleasant as punch. A real good egg. Not like that. Not like we saw. Becky, what were all those statues and carvings and things? No. Wait. Don't tell me. I know what they are."

"You do?"

"That's hoodoo. I know it. And if we get found out, Becky, we're not going to be able to stop it. We'll be baked in," Martha stuttered, her eyes wide.

"Let's not talk about this here. I know a place where we can go that's safer. But I've got to get something to drink. You holding any cabbage? I've got fifteen cents." Becky frowned.

"I think I can match that." Martha managed a smile.

They each bought a bottle of Coca-Cola and split a moon pie, leaving them enough for a couple of real drinks later. But after they ate and Martha drove a few miles toward downtown Savannah, she had to pull the car over. Becky threw up. She didn't want to tell Martha how scared she was and how sorry for dragging her into this mess.

"I should have listened to that man at the Crazy Calico and left well enough alone," Becky said before spitting on the ground.

"And I shouldn't have dyed my hair blonde for New Year's Eve last year." Martha patted Becky's arm. "We can't go around regretting every bad decision we ever made. Besides, some of those bad decisions were the best times we ever had together."

Becky grinned. "I'm sorry, Martha. I should have gone alone."

"What? So you could have all the great stories and adventures? Look, if you know a safe place to talk, let's get there. But don't think for one second that I'm sorry I came with you. If I didn't want to go, do you think I would have?"

"Yes, because I can be very pushy." Becky grinned again.

"That's true." Martha revved the engine and drove into downtown Savannah and the one-half address on Bryn Mawr Street.

CHAPTER FIFTEEN

*I*t was as if Becky and Martha had come inside Madame Cecelia's store covered in cobwebs. Ophelia dashed over to them. Swatting a kerchief all over their bodies, she muttered something in a language that definitely was not French and then glared at Becky.

"What have you been up to?"

"Us?" Becky batted her eyelashes. "Nothing much."

"You are covered in it. Get upstairs before more follows you in," Ophelia ordered and pushed both of them toward the stairs.

Becky took Martha's hand and led her to the back of the store and upstairs. There was only one man in the whole place. He looked up casually to check out their gams as they went up the stairs and then went back to his own business.

"What is this place?" Martha asked.

"You'll be pleasantly surprised as soon as we get upstairs. But watch out for Mimi. She's trouble." Becky smirked, feeling better the second she stepped across the threshold to Madame Cecelia's store.

Cecelia opened the door before Becky could knock and yanked both women inside. "Oh, you've really put us behind the eight ball on this one."

"I'm sorry. I didn't know where else to go," Becky pleaded before looking at Martha. "You remember Madame Cecelia from your party?"

"I…do. Madame Cecelia, it's nice to see you again."

"You, too, Martha. I do hope that nice boy who was stabbed in your home hasn't decided to linger," Cecelia said as if she were inquiring about a pie plate she had left behind.

"Not that I'm aware of," Martha replied meekly.

"Good. I can only deal with one crisis at a time. Now, the two of you need to have the sprinklers turned on you like a bulldog that found a mud puddle," Cecelia said. "Strip."

"What?" Martha gasped, crossing her arms across her breasts.

"Just do as she says, Martha," Becky urged. "It'll be for the best."

"I'm sorry, but one episode of indecent exposure per day is enough for me." She looked at Cecelia. "Not that it's any of your business, but I had to change in the back seat of my car as Becky drove. Have you ever been in a car when Becky is driving? Most people haven't because of an incident…"

"Would you quit flapping your gums and do as the lady tells you? Sheesh," Becky interrupted while she pulled her dress over her head and stood in the middle of Cecelia's apartment in her slip and stockings.

"I mean everything," Cecelia ordered as she stomped across the room and opened a small closet. She pulled out two silk robes. One was red with bright-green palm leaves all over it. The other was blue with white cranes. "Put these on."

Becky hurried behind a screen in the furthest corner of the living room and tossed her remaining clothes out before emerging in the blue robe. She stared at Martha, jerked her head toward the screen, and pointed with her thumb. Her friend huffed before stomping across the room to do the same.

"Mother, you'll take care of these?" Cecelia asked.

Ophelia had appeared in the doorway without

anyone noticing. Martha jumped and let out a squeal at the woman's sudden appearance.

"They should be burned," Ophelia said before spitting on the clothes.

"Oh no you don't. That is one of my favorite dresses. I danced with Nicholas Hendricks in that dress. One of the best nights of my life," Martha gushed. "He said he never met anyone who could dance the way I did."

"That was because that dress snaps in the front, and you hadn't noticed it had come undone," Becky replied.

"It was love at first sight," Martha cooed to her new audience.

"At least lust," Becky teased.

"That was the last time I ever saw him." Dramatically, Martha put her hand to her cheek and stared into space.

"He's not dead. He joined the Navy," Becky interrupted. "He's stationed in San Diego, California. Probably has a girl in every port along the way."

"You two need to shut up!" Ophelia ordered. "You bring in this filth and then blah-blah-blah, you give me headache, too."

Before Becky or Martha could reply, Ophelia

slipped out the door with every stitch of clothing they'd had on.

"Now we have to clean up the rest of you," Cecelia said.

Within minutes, Becky and Martha had each been nearly drowned in the kitchen sink as one at a time Cecelia washed their hair with special herbs and oil. Then she made them scrub their skin with a rough pumice stone, not letting them finish until their skin was red.

After a thorough inspection, she sat back in her chair by the window, shuffled her tarot cards, and told them to take a seat.

"Do you want to tell me how you got covered with all that?" Cecelia asked.

"Covered with what? I didn't see anything. Do I need to check my pockets to make sure my money hasn't been stolen?" Martha squawked.

"Of course not," Becky said and began to tell Cecelia about what she had seen and heard at the Tobin house that first night she went alone. "Mr. Tobin went stomping off into the woods. I wanted to see what he was hiding back there. Turns out he's brewing moonshine."

"But there was something odd about the still," Martha added as she tugged at the hem of her robe.

"There were all kinds of strange statues and jars of stuff all over the place. That was surely hoodoo if I had to guess. I'd hate to hear a fellow who was drinking that shine got mixed up and took a swig from one of those mason jars. Lord knows what would end up in his gullet."

"Didn't I tell you to leave all that alone?" Cecelia snapped. "Now you've gone and done it. Both of you. And I am not sure that I can help you."

"What are you talking about? Do you know what those trinkets and jars are?" Becky asked.

"Like your friend said. That's hoodoo," Cecelia said as she slowly laid out her cards on the table. "Hoodoo is a black magic. It is the blackest magic that revolves around decay and death. Like maggots, it feasts on what remains. It gathers its power from those things that normal people want to avoid."

"Like cemeteries?" Becky breathed.

Cecelia nodded sadly.

"So what does that have to do with you sticking us in the dunk tank?" Martha asked. "And where are our clothes?"

"You were covered with a dust. Like you can tell a bee has visited so many flowers when its body is covered with pollen. That's how you two looked,"

Cecelia said, looking down at her cards for a second and then back at her guests.

"Eww." Martha grimaced.

"What does that do? Why would we be covered in that? We didn't touch anyone or anything," Becky replied before nervously chewing her lip.

"The person practicing the hoodoo obviously has coated the area with it. Let's say it's the same as a cop putting a tail on you. Wherever you go, you leave a trail behind you for them to follow," Cecelia said. "But once again, you surprise me. You ladies wore disguises and jumped in a car. What was on your clothes when you got to me probably wasn't nearly as much as what was on the clothes you had worn into the woods."

"That's a relief," Martha sighed.

"How do you know what hoodoo is?" Cecelia asked with a sly grin on her face, her right eyebrow arching high.

"We had a maid when I was a little girl who told me about it. Said her great-grandmother, who was still alive at the time, practiced it. I don't know if that was true or not, but she told me that if you do hoodoo, you do the devil's work." Martha nodded. "I always thought that was catchy, so it stuck with me."

"Becky? Are you all right?" Cecelia asked.

Martha looked at her friend. "Becky, my gosh, gal, what is it?"

Becky looked at Martha with tears in her eyes. When Martha took Becky's hands in hers, she could feel them shaking.

"I went to that house by myself. If I walked through all that pollen, that means I led them back home. I led them right through the tobacco fields and back to my house. I have to get back there right away." Becky jumped up from her seat, nearly tipping over the table.

"Wait, you can't run outside in a robe." Martha held her hands tightly.

"I'll run naked if I have to. Mama and Daddy don't know. They won't know what hit them if I don't try and warn them, or maybe I can make things right." Becky pulled her hands away. "What can I do? Tell me. I'll do anything."

"Don't say that. You make a promise to do anything, and someone may just take you up on that offer," Ophelia replied as she once again seemed to appear out of thin air. Their clothes were in her hands. She tossed one bundle to Martha, who dashed behind the screen, telling Becky all the way that she was not to leave without her.

"What can I do? What can I do to make sure they

don't hurt my parents?" Becky pleaded to Ophelia. "Will you help me?"

"There isn't anything we can do," she said flatly.

"But that doesn't mean the hoodoo woman will do anything. You wait until the dust settles. Stop going over there or anywhere near the Ruthmeyer remains. Mother and I will put our heads together. Maybe we can find someone who can help," Cecelia said.

Becky took her clothes from Ophelia and slipped behind the screen after Martha had come out, adjusting her dress and stepping into her shoes.

"I refuse to believe there isn't anything that can be done," she squawked over the screen to Becky. "Even the mob is afraid of the D.A. Everyone has a weakness."

"They know Becky's. Now it's up to us to find theirs," Cecelia said.

No one saw Becky behind the screen as she got dressed. She was glad. The last thing she wanted was for everyone to see her crying.

CHAPTER SIXTEEN

*B*y the time Martha had driven Becky back to the Mackenzie plantation, the sun was setting. Ophelia had taken the clothes the women had worn on the Tobin property and thrown them all into the hungry, white-hot incinerator underneath the apothecary. Becky had hardly said a word the entire trip. Martha suggested getting out and tossing a few back just to clear their heads.

"Come on. We'll throw on some new duds, a little munitions on our cheeks, and find the first sharp-shooter to come along at Willie's. Get the blood flowing a little, Beck, and I'll bet we'll come up with a swell idea to help throw some ice on this inferno," Martha pleaded, but Becky just looked out at the long lines of tobacco plants on her father's land. She squinted off into the distance.

"Do you hear that?" Becky asked.

Martha tilted her head and listened. Her shoulders fell, her eyes widened, and her mouth fell open.

"Well, I guess the party has come to you. Why didn't you tell me Judge and Kitty were planning to trip the light fantastic?" Martha smirked.

"Did you really just use that ancient term? You sound like my grandmother." Becky shook her head. "Of all the nights. I'm going to be Edisoned to death. No matter who is here, Kitty has already told them I need a beau. Let the Spanish Inquisition begin."

"It won't be all bad," Martha said as she pulled up to see more than half a dozen cars parked in the front of the house.

"Oh, no? That's the Penbrokes' bus." Becky pointed to a large behemoth of a Ford. "They have a son our age. Mama is probably fitting me for handcuffs as we speak. Wedding dates are being tossed around. And I'm sure he's already gotten more than an eyeful of Fanny. That sounds rather obscene now that I say it out loud."

"Don't worry, Rebecca Madeline Mackenzie. I'll be your escort tonight. However, if your father is making his famous Manhattans, I can't promise I won't be all in by the time your honeymoon has been planned."

"You're a real pal," Becky replied.

Once they were out of the car and coming up the front steps, Kitty appeared with a drink in her hand. Her hair was in perfect finger waves, as it always was, and she was wearing the new dress she'd picked out for herself when they had all gone downtown shopping. She smiled at Martha but gave Becky a stern look.

"Why, Miss Bourdeaux, I should have known my one and only child would be with you. What have you two ladies been up to?" Kitty asked, trying not to raise her voice.

Becky knew her mother well, and had there not been a crowd of people, Kitty would have read Becky *and* Martha the Riot Act.

"You know us, Kitty. Just a couple of angels with dirty faces," Martha teased, making Kitty chuckle.

"Becky, Mr. Stephen Penbroke is here to see you." Kitty smiled deviously. "Why don't you sneak upstairs and freshen up before I make formal introductions?"

"Okay, Mama," Becky replied without fuss.

Her mother instantly knew something was wrong.

175

"I'll have her spit polished in no time, Kitty," Martha replied, pushing Becky up the stairs before anyone could see them.

"I can't do this tonight," Becky whined.

"What are you talking about? Tonight is the exact night you need to do this. Hi, Fanny," Martha said as they pushed past Fanny on the stairs.

"Well, look what the cat dragged in. Becky, I was afraid I'd have to do all the entertaining for the entire evening without you here. You know how everyone enjoys your sense of humor. If nothing else, you do have that." Fanny grinned.

"I've also got a size-seven shoe that will fit perfectly up your..."

"We'll be down in a jiffy, Fanny," Martha interrupted Becky before she could finish her sentence. Without thinking, she grabbed Becky's hand and pulled her into her room, shutting the door quickly behind them.

"I'm going to bed. Maybe all this is just a bad dream, and I'll wake up with nothing more than Fanny to give me the heebie-jeebies." Becky crawled onto her bed only to have Martha poke her in the ribs.

"It's not a dream, and you are not going to bed. There's a fella down there who wants to talk to you."

Martha stomped to Becky's closet and began flipping through her dresses. She grabbed a dark-brown number with a drop waist that had black beads sewn in for extra sparkle. "When did you get this? Wear it. Put it on this instant, or so help me, I'll have Fanny pick out your dress."

Becky looked at Martha and narrowed her eyes. "Maybe you're right." Becky sighed.

"Of course I am. Here's the scoop. If the Tobins and their witch are going to try and pull a fast one, sitting and waiting for it to happen isn't going to stop it. So have a drink. Let your mind get a little fuzzy. Then tomorrow, we'll look at it all with clear, hungover heads."

"You really are a good egg, Martha." Becky wrapped her arms around her friend's neck and squeezed.

"And if we live through this, I want that dress." Martha tugged on Becky's hem, making her laugh.

Within ten minutes, both girls were primped and looking very pretty as they greeted the guests.

"Rebecca, Becky, honey, there is someone I want you to meet," Kitty said as she walked up to her daughter with a fresh drink in her hand. She took her daughter by the hand, causing Becky to take

Martha by the hand, and in a three-person train, they wove through the crowd to the back porch.

"Who is that tall drink of water?" Martha whispered.

"Beats me." Becky shrugged.

At the edge of the porch, a tall man with naturally wavy blond hair and deep-green eyes was talking with Fanny.

"France sounds wonderful." His voice was deep and a little scratchy, making Martha squeeze Becky's hand. "I might have to take a trip there someday."

"Stephen?" Kitty called. "I'm so sorry to interrupt, Fanny."

"That's quite all right, Aunt Kitty. I'm sure I was just boring Stephen to death," Fanny gushed as she pushed up her cleavage and shrugged her shoulders.

"Not at all. I'd love to hear more about your trip to Paris at another time," he said politely as Kitty pulled Becky along.

"He shouldn't have said that," Martha whispered to Becky. "She's going to pounce on him like a cat on a mouse."

Becky started to chuckle, but as soon as Stephen's eyes met hers, she coughed and regained her composure.

"Stephen Penbroke, this is my daughter Rebecca.

I think the last time you two saw each other, you couldn't have been more than five years old," Kitty cooed. "And Becky, do you know that you told me you were going to marry Stephen?"

"Mama! What kind of thing is that to say? I'm sorry, Stephen. My mother has obviously let the evening go to her head," Becky said, rolling her eyes. "We've talked about having her committed, but so far none of the sanitariums are willing to take her. I guess they have a limit on how much crazy they'll accept."

Stephen laughed out loud as Fanny gasped. Kitty, looking slyly at Becky, kissed her daughter on the cheek before turning to leave.

"Kitty, can you get me one of those drinks you're having?" Martha asked as she linked her arm through Kitty's. "Fanny, why don't you join us? You look like you're running a little dry."

Fanny looked at Stephen and batted her eyes and flipped her bouncy blonde locks behind her shoulders. "Don't go anywhere. I'll be right back."

Becky cleared her throat as Stephen watched Fanny sashay into the house behind Kitty and Martha.

"I thought she'd never leave." Stephen sighed.

"Really? Most of the men Mama tries to fix me up

with are very happy Fanny is here. I'm just a stop along the way to the berry patch." Becky folded her arms across her chest. Why hadn't Martha offered to get her a drink?

"I don't believe that," Stephen said.

"Look, just because I live on a tobacco farm doesn't mean I'm some apple-knocker. And I'm not looking to get married. Kitty is looking for me to get married, but I've got other plans," Becky huffed. "So forgive me for being a wet blanket, but this bank's closed."

"You are just like I remember you. Even when we were little kids, you were the one who stood out the most. Do you still go to the cemetery?" Stephen innocently asked.

"What?" Becky took a step closer.

"When you were a little girl, I quite clearly remember you used to like to play in the cemetery out behind your daddy's fields. You used to pretend you could talk to the people buried there," he said with twinkling eyes.

"I do like to go out there sometimes just to get a little privacy. Walk and smell the fresh air," Becky replied, making no mention that she did indeed talk with the people buried there.

"Maybe you'd give me a tour," Stephen said.

"Maybe," Becky replied.

They stood and talked on the back porch for some time until Stephen made a bold suggestion.

"I've noticed you haven't had a single drink. How about it? Something to wet your whistle?" Stephen smiled as he ascended the steps directly in front of Becky, standing dangerously close and looking up at her with a sly grin.

There was something in those big green eyes that told Becky she might be in trouble. But it was the best kind of trouble, and after the day she'd had, she was ready to forget about *today* all together.

"I'll take anything with ice in it," Becky replied.

Before she had a second to take a deep breath, Martha was at her side.

"What is that?" Martha gushed.

"What is what?"

"That big cat that's been chewing your ear off since we got here." Martha smirked. "Don't tell me that Kitty found her daughter a suitable beau?"

"I'm talking with the fella and being polite. That's all." Becky tried not to smile.

"Rebecca Madeline Mackenzie," Martha whispered, "you act as if we just met. I know that look, and I know that stance, and I know everything about you. You can't hide it from me. You are smitten."

"I am not."

"Yes you are. And I think it's wonderful. He's a Southerner. He comes from a line of good stock. He's easy on the eyes and has a voice that could snap your garters."

"Martha! I'm shocked at you. Talking like that when everyone knows you and Teddy are destined to be together. You shouldn't be ogling the guests."

"Teddy," Martha sighed.

"What? Don't tell me there's trouble in paradise? When did this happen?"

"I'll give you one guess." Martha pinched her lips together.

"I should have known I'd find you two out here. Where's Stephen?" Fanny replied before she started laughing. "Don't tell me you scared him away already, Becky. My, you certainly do have a way with the gents."

Before Becky could say anything back to Fanny, she heard Judge shouting at the other end of the house.

Without thinking, she walked into the house. With each step, it seemed like the conversation was getting quieter, the music was slowing, and everyone was collectively holding their breath. As she made her way to the front parlor, she saw people gathered at the windows.

Through the front screen door, she saw her father's tall, strong silhouette. She walked to the door, pulled it open, and stepped alongside her father only to see that they had a party crasher: Mr. Earl Tobin.

CHAPTER SEVENTEEN

*B*ecky could feel her heart racing. Had he followed the "dust" Cecelia said she and Martha had been covered in? Had she led this man directly to her front door?

"Mr. Tobin, I'm not sure what all this is about, but I'd be honored if you'd come into my home and join me for a drink. We've got plenty of ice, and my wife did bake the most delicious peach pie for the occasion. Would you...?"

"Don't try giving me the high hat," Earl Tobin growled.

"Mr. Tobin, I assure you that I'm not," Judge replied firmly. "We're neighbors."

"I know what people are saying around town and in your fields about that no-good Ruthmeyer's house burning down. You were there, weren't you? You were trying to save that no-good chiseler," Mr. Tobin hissed.

He looked as if he'd scrambled through the brush himself to get to the Mackenzie home. His brown pants were dirty and torn at the knees. His shirt was dirty from sweat, and the undershirt that showed at his collar had spots on it. His skin was slick with sweat, making Becky think he had run all the way to their front porch.

"Mr. Tobin," Judge said, "you are well aware that my property butted up against Mr. Ruthmeyer's. When we saw smoke, we didn't think to ponder whose property it was. We went to help."

"But if it were my property, would you have jumped so fast?" Mr. Tobin asked.

"Of course," Judge replied.

It was obvious to Becky that Mr. Tobin had no idea who her father was. He would never turn away a person who needed help. He had built his fortune with his own two hands and had known hard times. Many people had turned their noses up at him before he bought his first acre. Many nights he had gone to bed hungry. But that hadn't stopped him.

"Well, smell you. I know what you think of me. And I know what all of you have been saying about my wife." He pointed at everyone on the porch. Becky looked him right in the eyes, but he didn't act like he recognized her.

"Mr. Tobin, what goes on between a man and his wife is no one else's business. I can assure you that there has been no such discussion in this house. Now, I want you to state your business or get off my land." Judge stared at Mr. Tobin without flinching. It was Mr. Tobin who blinked first.

Becky's heart took comfort in that until she saw movement behind Mr. Tobin. It was off in the distance a piece, but it was there. Becky was sure she was looking at Leelee. The woman with the scarf wrapped around her head was back there. Becky left her father's side to go to the corner of the porch and look. Mr. Tobin paid no attention to her. She stared hard into the darkness and saw the mysterious woman.

Leelee was crawling on her hands and knees like a dog looking for a place to relieve itself, back and forth, back and forth, until suddenly she stopped. After folding herself onto her knees, she looked in Becky's direction and pointed a long, bony arm.

Becky squared her shoulders and stared back. Her heart was racing, but she wasn't going to show any fear. She couldn't. If Becky was the reason Mr.

Tobin was here, and there was no thinking otherwise, then she was going to have to face the music—or, like Cecelia had said, find their weakness. But that was going to be easier said than done.

"I've bought up what's left of Ruthmeyer's property. That's my property now. I hold the bank note that says so. If anyone from this here plantation thinks they can set foot on my property, they'll find themselves in a Chicago overcoat. I mean anybody, even that daughter of yours. I've heard she's a snoop and claims she talks to ghosts. Sounds like a candidate for the booby-hatch, if you ask me," he hissed before spitting on the ground.

"Mr. Tobin, you've made your point. Now get off my land, or you'll be on the receiving end of my shotgun."

Several of the men at the party, including Stephen Penbroke, stepped up and stood by Judge in support.

Becky looked to her mother, who was standing in the doorway. She was embarrassed by what Mr. Tobin had said about her. Her mother tried so hard to have Becky blend in. But Becky didn't feel as scared as she had that afternoon. She was angry.

"You think you can threaten me?" Mr. Tobin shouted. "You don't know who you're dealing with!

If you think I'm scared of the likes of you, you couldn't be more wrong! I'm saying now to all these folks here that Judge Mackenzie comes from a no-good family, and I'll beat you like a dog if you set one foot on my property! Like a dog!" He was like a wild animal.

"And I'm telling you to get off my land, or I'll have you thrown off!" Judge shouted, his voice echoing over the field. Becky was sure she heard the rustling of the tobacco leaves from her father's booming voice.

Earl Tobin sneered and pointed at Judge. He muttered something under his breath and swaggered off into the darkness. Becky watched him and waited for Leelee to join him, but she never did. She had disappeared, and he walked alone somewhere.

"I'm sorry about that, folks," Judge said. "Everyone, refill your glasses, and crank up that Victrola, Kitty. It's early, and we've still got another two or three neighbors to pay us a visit."

Everyone laughed, and within minutes, the entire crowd had forgotten about Earl Tobin. Everyone but Becky.

"Daddy?" She took her father by his sleeve and pulled him toward her.

"Becky, don't you fret yourself over what that

man says," Judge said, smoothing Becky's hair. "He drinks his own moonshine. He's not right in his head. I'm sure he believes the world is out to get him, and now that his favorite enemy is gone, he's got to find a new one."

"You know he brews moonshine?" Becky asked. "How do you know that?"

"Oh, some of the people around town have mentioned it," Judge replied.

"The same people that say his wife was having an affair with Mr. Ruthmeyer?"

"Some of them." Judge smiled but looked sad. "Not everyone has things as good as we do. Mr. Tobin isn't a bad man. He's just lost. It's unfortunate." Judge looked at his daughter. "That's a pretty dress."

"Martha picked it out for me. Daddy, I saw Mr. Tobin's moonshine still. I went looking, and I think he knows it was me who was out there." Becky felt a wave of relief wash over her as she unloaded the burden, hoping that might help the situation.

"Now what in the world would make you do such a fool thing? Becky, those moonshiners are not gentlemen. You might as well have found the man's life savings in cash dollars—that's how they view that white lightning. Had he been in an intoxicated state of mind, he could have killed you." Judge frowned. "Well, I guess it's too late to make amends. Mr. Tobin seemed to be rather agitated, and I don't think anything would have appeased him."

"I saw some strange things over there." Becky started to speak, but Stephen Penbroke sauntered up to Judge with his hand extended.

"Mr. Mackenzie, might I borrow Becky for just a few minutes?"

"By all means, Stephen," Judge said, shaking Stephen's hand before giving Becky a gentle nudge and leaving to join Kitty inside the house.

"Well, that was some show," Stephen said. "Yeah. Well, you know how men who drink their own home brew can be. It pickles the brain."

Becky gave a chuckle, still looking out where she'd seen Leelee.

"Would you like to go somewhere quiet to talk?" Stephen asked.

"I don't think there's a quiet corner in the house." Becky smiled.

Just then, Martha came out of the house in a whirlwind.

"Was that really Mr. Tobin ranting and raving out here? My Lord, I held my breath the entire time and tried not to be seen. Did he recognize you? Do you think he knew it was us? Why was he up here? What did he think Judge was going to do?" Martha finally took a gulp of air.

"It was him, but he didn't recognize anyone. Or if he did, he was good at pretending," Becky said then forced a pleasant smile. "Have you met Stephen Penbroke? This is my dearest friend and partner in crime, Martha Bourdeaux."

"Hello, Miss Bourdeaux." Stephen took her hand and brought it to his lips.

"Call me Martha." She giggled.

The familiar honking of Teddy's jalopy cut through the night as he pulled up onto a vacant slot of grass. Becky looked at Martha, who was busy tittering over Stephen's attention. He certainly was a big-timer.

"What's this? Rebecca Mackenzie, are you trying to have a rub without me?" Teddy asked before stopping dead in his tracks as he caught sight of Stephen holding Martha's hand.

Becky rolled her eyes. Martha and Teddy were two peas in a pod but insisted on keeping it platonic. They danced around their feelings for each other like two fireflies on a summer breeze.

"What's eating you?" Martha replied, smiling.

"Listen, skirt, if there's a shindig going on at this

dive, I better be on the bank roll." Teddy smiled, but he was obviously sizing up Stephen without trying to be obvious.

"Who ruffled your feathers?" Becky asked. "Of course you are. Will the rest of the Rockdale clan be joining us?"

"They're bringing up the caboose." Teddy jerked his thumb over his shoulder.

Becky quickly made introductions before Martha began recounting the excitement Teddy had just missed.

"Really? Old man Tobin? That guy is a loose wire," Teddy replied.

"What do you say we blow this pop stand?" Becky suggested. "I could use a change of scenery and a little whoopee. This place is filled with fire extinguishers."

"That sounds like a great idea. Mind if I tag along?" Stephen asked, looking only at Becky.

"Sure, if you don't mind being like sardines in my flivver." Teddy winked at Martha, who looked in the other direction.

Then, as if by teleportation, Fanny showed up.

"Did I hear y'all saying you're leaving? Can you make room for me to squeeze in?" And *she* looked only at Teddy and Stephen.

"The more the merrier," Teddy replied, grabbing Martha by the hand as if snatching her away from Stephen before he could make a move.

But Stephen was busy slipping his arm around Becky and gently guiding her toward the car. Becky was shocked but allowed him to cuddle her, if for no other reason than to annoy Fanny. It was going to be a long night.

CHAPTER EIGHTEEN

"There's plenty of room back here, Stephen," Fanny said. "There's no need for you to cram yourself into the rumble seat."

"I've been stuffed in worse places. So where are we going?" he asked, looking at Becky.

She felt her cheeks blush. She hated to admit that Stephen was a breath of fresh air. He knew so little about her except what Mr. Tobin had said. That was enough to keep Becky from looking him in the eye. Had Adam been there, he would have stomped up to Earl Tobin and, hoodoo or not, socked him right in the kisser. As it was, no one else really came to her defense. Just Judge.

"Yeah, Becky, where are we going?" Teddy hadn't let go of Martha's hand since the engine started.

"Martha, why don't you pick," Becky said.

"Oh, dear. No offense, Martha, but you picked the Crazy Calico, and that didn't turn out very well for anyone," Fanny said. "That poor Mr. Loomis barely recovered. He is sweet on Becky, in case you weren't aware."

"Oh, I didn't know you had a fella." Stephen smirked.

The idea that Becky might have had a crush didn't seem to bother him. In fact, the way he leaned in toward her made Becky think that made her seem all the more appealing.

"I don't. Hugh Loomis is a friend of my mother's," Becky replied, still looking out into the night. She was enjoying the air and the wind in her face and couldn't wait to get to some noisy place where the music was too loud to talk and the only thing to do was get a wiggle on with some giggle water.

"Oh, Becky. Don't be so silly," Fanny continued. "The only reason poor Hugh even drank that moonshine was to impress you. He was making doll eyes at her all night."

"He was making crossed eyes at everyone after his first sip of that shine," Martha replied as she turned around in her seat to face her fellow travelers. "I'll bet my life he was seeing double. Hey, Teddy."

"Yes, my darling?"

"How's about we take a jaunt to that dive over by that place. You know what I'm talking about?" Martha said.

"You mean that one place that has the thing?" Teddy replied.

"Yes, with that other thing they have next to the giant clock." Martha clapped her hands and nodded.

"That's a swell idea. Hold on to your hats, folks. We're heading to that one place."

Teddy hit the gas, and in a short while, everyone was spilling out of the car and making tracks to a plain wooden door on the side of a warehouse. Within minutes, they were inside the building, and Becky had already disappeared on the dance floor.

"Where did she go?" Stephen asked Martha as they made their way to a booth with velvet cushions around a small table.

"I hate to break it to you, Romeo, but Becky's dance card is full. Every sheik who can keep up wants to swing her around the floor," Martha replied. "Plus, she's dizzy about someone, and it ain't Hugh Loomis."

"Dizzy? With who?" Stephen didn't look the least

bit shocked or even slightly disturbed that Martha was giving him the brush-off for Becky. It annoyed her that he looked rather amused.

"Now don't go getting in a lather. He's a big-six by the name of Adam White. I'm giving you the straight dope. You seem like a good egg, and I think it's only fair that you know." Martha smiled. "But if it's any consolation, you can certainly take home the booby prize."

Fanny, who had captured the attention of every man in the place with her slow walk and sleepy eyes, slunk up to the table with a drink in her hand.

"This place reminds me of one of the many evenings I was out in Paris. Oh, the nightlife in Paris is so much different from the United States. Especially the South. I'm not saying it's better—my, no. I'm just saying that there are little niceties that the Parisians expect that Americans would just never think of," Fanny gushed as she slid into the booth next to Martha.

Teddy arrived with drinks for everyone. Becky made an appearance long enough to throw her drink back and get back on the dance floor. Each time she did, she had a different partner, until finally, the band slowed things down, and Stephen made his move.

"How about it? Care to dance, or will I be leaving here with sore toes?" he teased, hitting Becky in the ego.

"I ain't no corn masher." She smiled back and accepted. But as soon as he swung her onto the dance floor, she felt his strong arms tighten around her and felt his soft, shaved cheek pressed against hers.

"I didn't think I'd get a chance to talk to you alone," he said tenderly in her ear.

"We're hardly alone," Becky replied.

"Don't be a dumb Dora. You know what I mean," Stephen scoffed.

"Dumb Dora? Who do you think you're talking to?" Becky pulled back only to feel him hold her tighter. It wasn't painful like when Edward at the Crazy Calico had squeezed her. No, this was nice. Exciting and dangerous.

"Becky Mackenzie, I've been waiting for you since I was five years old. You didn't really notice me then. But I think you notice me now," he said in her ear, making her shiver and blush.

"I think you're a swell guy, Stephen. But it's obvious that Fanny's got her sights set on you," Becky replied.

"Well, let's just say I was never all that crazy about Paris."

Stephen picked Becky up and swung her around, and when her feet hit the floor and the music changed, he danced her breath away. And Becky was thankful for it. She wanted to forget about moonshine and Leelee with the scarf around her head and Mr. Tobin the party crasher. They sounded like characters out of a dime-store mystery novel. And it was a mystery. What were they up to? Why were they picking on Daddy and his land now? Was it really because of Becky snooping around?

Stop! You're here to have fun and forget about the world for a little while! You've got this big brute sweeping you all over the floor. The liquor is wet and the ice is cold. There is nothing to worry about in here, she argued with herself.

If Judge didn't seem too worried, you shouldn't be worried either. But Judge hadn't seen the woman digging in the bone yard. And he didn't see the men with their boiled eyes and lips sewn shut. He didn't see the statues or hear what they did to Mr. Gavin. Stop! Stop! Stop!

Suddenly Becky's head was swimming.

"Beck? Are you okay?" Stephen asked, holding her in his arms.

"I don't know. I feel like someone slipped me a mickey," she replied, putting her hand to her head.

"Hey, what's eating you?" Martha, who had been watching them dance and taking special joy in pointing out their talent to Fanny, rushed up to them.

"I don't know. I think I'm just tired," Becky replied.

"A little fresh air will do her some good." Martha slapped Stephen's shoulder. "Would you mind, Big and Good-lookin'? She's had a long day."

"Not at all."

Stephen kept his arm around Becky's waist and led her through the crowd and out the door. The cool, fresh air hit her like a shot in the arm. Becky took a deep breath and hung onto Stephen's arm.

"Here. Take a load off." He lifted her by the waist and sat her down gently on the hood of an old Fiat.

"I'm feeling better." She put her hand to her cheek. "I usually don't get that way. I love to dance. But something's gone to my head. I've had one of those days that you wish you could wrap up in paper and ship back in the mail."

"Do you want to talk about it?" Stephen asked, leaning close but not too close.

She looked at his hands. They were clean and

smooth. He obviously worked with his head and not his hands.

"I don't think you'd find it all that interesting." All Becky needed was Stephen Penbroke reporting back to his mother that she was having run-ins with the local loony moonshiner while his maid was stealing dirt from her cemetery and practicing hoodoo on people. That would make it back to Kitty before she could say "amen." The lecture she'd get would be one for the books.

"Sure I would. If I could sit through an hour of Fanny's trip to Paris, I can certainly listen to something from a dame like you."

He was a charmer. His blond hair had curled even tighter with sweat from dancing, and his green eyes crinkled when he smiled.

"A dame like me?"

"Yeah. You're a ripe tomato, and I mean that with all due respect." He winked.

"Horse feathers. There isn't a gent in the place who's noticed anyone but Fanny since she walked in. The sad thing is the same goes at my homestead." Becky didn't mean to whine, but Stephen had asked, and now she was singing like a canary.

"Let me tell you something about the male species," Stephen said. "We like to look at things.

Pretty things. Things that are soft all over and smile and bat their eyes. But when it comes down to it, there is nothing better than a girl with a good head on her shoulders. Sure, some palookas would rather have the jewelry hanging from their arm. But we're talking real big shots. The kind that carry a violin case around with them." Stephen put his index finger next to his nose.

"You seem to know a lot about it." Becky leaned back and put her hands on her hips. "Don't tell me your hands are so soft because you're a can opener."

Stephen laughed. "I don't crack safes or skulls. I just know about them. I read the papers like everyone else. I also know that dishes like Fanny come a dime a dozen. But dames like you...well, that's a horse of a completely different color."

Becky blushed and took another deep breath. At the mention of newspapers, she thought about Adam, and a twinge of guilt plucked at her heart. What was there to feel guilty about? She'd danced with other fellas before, and Adam even let them cut in on occasion. Besides, she'd known Stephen when she was five years old. Not that she remembered at all, but it only made sense that they would get along since they came from the same kind of families and had such deep roots in the South.

"I think it's about time we blow," Becky said.

"Are you sure? Not just one more dance?" he tempted.

"Maybe another time." Becky resisted, feeling proud of herself. Stephen Penbroke was nothing special. He wasn't like Adam. He was nothing at all like Adam. Maybe that was why she was fighting the urge to kiss him.

CHAPTER NINETEEN

*A*s soon as they walked back into the speakeasy to collect Teddy, Martha, and Fanny, Becky heard her name being called.

"Becky! Over here!"

It was a male voice, and for a second, she panicked. Was it Adam, and was he going to grill her about what she had been doing outside with Stephen? But when she saw the man waving, she not only sighed with relief but smiled happily.

"Count Ernesto!" She waved back. "What a nice surprise. How's tricks?"

Count Ernesto was a tall, glamorous-looking man who looked like he might have just stepped foot off a ship that had sailed to half a dozen exotic locations. His skin was tanned, and dark ringlets hung around his face. He wore a gray vest over a light-gray button-down shirt, and his trousers were frayed around the edges like those of so many men who worked hard for a living. He towered over Becky, and she once again noticed his long, thin fingers that looked as if they belonged on an artist's hands. When she had first met him, he had been pulling roses and scarves out of thin air for a group of gasping ladies at Martha's birthday party.

"Becky, I've been looking all over for you," he said, slipping his hand around her elbow. "Excuse us just a second," he said to Stephen, who looked as if he was ready to pounce. Becky quickly made introductions.

"I'll just be a second," Becky said to Stephen, who nodded and went to join Martha, Teddy, and Fanny.

"What's on the agenda, Count?" Becky smiled but soon realized Count Ernesto wasn't there to have a good time. When he'd said he was looking all over for her, he meant it literally.

"Madam Cecelia's store was vandalized," he said sadly.

"What?"

"A couple of goons in overalls and dirty shirts,

like they slept in the woods all night, came calling. They kicked the door in and smashed the front window."

"Did they say what they wanted?" Becky clutched her throat.

"They said they wanted the young men who were spying on them before they ran to the apothecary. They think you and Martha are men?" Ernesto shrugged his shoulders.

"We wore disguises. When we went back in the woods to see what Mr. Tobin was up to, we wore men's clothes so we wouldn't ruin our own things. Oh, what have I done?" Becky wanted to cry. She looked over at Martha, who was watching with a worried look on her face.

"There was a woman sitting in their car," Ernesto continued.

"The black woman with the scarf around her head?" Becky interrupted.

"Well, yes, she was there. But there was another woman. Very fair, looked like a frail bird, and she was wearing a heavy coat even though it was a warm night," Ernesto continued.

"That had to be Mrs. Tobin. What was she doing?" Becky asked.

"She was sitting in the car with the motor

running, crying," Ernesto said. "She didn't look like she wanted any part of what was going on. But still, she didn't move or speak or even look up. She just grimaced."

"Are Cecelia and Ophelia all right? I should go to them." Becky rose to run to Teddy and beg him to take her across town, but Ernesto grabbed her arm first.

"They are okay. That's why they sent me looking for you. Cecelia wants you at the store in three days at midnight," Ernesto said. "In the meantime, you need to take this." He handed her a pouch made of gingham that held some trinkets inside. It had a long string around it that Becky instinctively put around her neck.

"What is this?" she asked.

"It isn't much. But it will protect you for a short while—at least until you see her in a couple nights. Remember, three nights from now. Midnight. Don't be late," Ernesto said with a sigh of relief. It was as if he'd unburdened himself of a heavy weight.

"Is it hoodoo?" Becky asked innocently.

"We can't protect you against that," Ernesto said sadly. "Cecelia knows a lot. Some people call her a witch. I call her a seer. But what she has is a gift that she uses as such. People who work in hoodoo, they've signed a contract with the evil forces that roam the Earth. They may not live any better than anyone else, but they'll live longer just to fulfill the evil that is asked of them. Please, keep this on at all times." He pointed to the small bag around her neck. "I'm not sure what it can do. Maybe it will just keep you invisible and protect you until the time comes."

"Protect me from what? The time comes for what?" Becky asked.

Ernesto didn't reply. Instead, he kissed her on the cheek and left. She didn't even get a chance to ask him about Adam. They worked alongside one another at the same printing press. Maybe that was because Adam was an afterthought. How could she think about him at a time like this? The only reason Mr. Tobin hadn't busted her in the chops tonight was because he didn't know she had been the one on his property. But now her friends were paying the price.

Becky walked back to the table where her friends had been sitting. Teddy was telling a story to a gent sitting next to him that was a real side-splitter, as they were both laughing and clapping each other on the back. Fanny had only lit up when she saw Stephen returning to the table and had latched onto him like a tick on a hound. It was Martha who was reading Becky's face and not liking the story it told.

"Are you all right?" Martha asked, climbing over Teddy to take Becky's hands. "You look like someone just walked over your grave."

"Oh, Martha. I think I've really made a mess of things." She told her what Ernesto had said. "You'd better get home, too. Even if they don't know it was us who were on their property, they are going to try and smoke us out. I'm afraid it might work if we aren't careful."

Martha swallowed hard.

"Here, take this." Becky removed the pouch of trinkets from her neck and put it around Martha's neck. "Ernesto said it will keep you invisible and safe until I can figure out what to do."

"If you are going to Cecelia's in three nights at midnight, I'm going with you," Martha said, squeezing Becky's hand.

"I can't let you do that. I've gotten you in enough trouble as it is," Becky said.

"Yes, and we almost burned down a school in eighth grade because we were smoking in the basement. If you think I'm going to leave you holding the bag just because the going is getting tough, you don't know me very well, Rebecca. I'll meet you there with bells on."

Becky leaned her forehead against Martha's. "You're the cat's pajamas, Martha."

"Birds of a feather, sweetheart," Martha replied.

CHAPTER TWENTY

It had been two days since Mr. Tobin had shown up at Becky's parents' house and threatened everyone. This morning she woke up early to a clear, blue sky and birds chirping on the trellis. As much as she tried not to think about him, Stephen had remained on her mind since they had gotten reacquainted. Still in her nightclothes, she climbed out of bed, took a seat at her desk by the bedroom window, and pulled out her sketchbook. She opened it to the last page she'd drawn on to see an almost perfect likeness of Stephen that she'd sketched from memory. She flipped back to the dozens of pictures she'd drawn of Adam and wondered what she was going to do about the two of them.

Nothing. You aren't going to do anything. Stephen is practically a stranger. Adam, he's anything but a stranger. And... She couldn't think of anything else.

She shook her head, slammed the book shut, and pushed her window open to get a breath of fresh air. As she leaned out, she saw one of Judge's field workers running like the devil was chasing him. Instantly, Becky knew something was wrong, and her breath caught in her throat. Without her robe, she dashed downstairs to meet the worker as he called for Judge.

"Mr. Mackenzie, sir. We've got a problem in the field," the man panted.

Becky knew him. He'd worked on their land for several years. The nice fellow by the name of Clemont, who was normally quite soft-spoken, was now drenched in sweat and looking concerned as Lucretia led him into the dining room.

"What's going on, Clemont?" Judge said, setting his paper down and pushing his coffee cup away.

"I ain't never seen nothin' like it. Looks like some kind of fungus or mold or something on the leaves of a good portion of crops," he said nervously, worrying the wide brim of his hat in his hand. "I ain't never seen anything like it."

"Daddy, is everything all right?" Becky interrupted.

"Morning, Becky. I'm sure everything will be fine. Show me what you're talking about, Clemont. Let's see what we can see." Judge stood from the table and followed Clemont out the back door.

Becky ran back upstairs, only to run into Fanny along the way. She was in a thick terrycloth robe and stared wide-eyed at Becky.

"My goodness, cousin. Did you just let that hired hand see you in such a state?" Fanny chuckled. "That's one way to attract the wrong kind of attention."

"You'd know all about that," Becky snapped back before hustling into her room, where she quickly dressed. She ran back downstairs. Her father and Clemont were just a few yards in front of her by the time she let the back door slam behind her. Before she broke a sweat, she was trotting next to her father, one of his long strides taking her two quick steps to keep up.

"Where'd you come from?" Judge smiled down at his daughter.

"Oh, I just want to see what Clemont is talking about," Becky said.

"You look worried," Judge replied.

All Becky could do was shrug. When they got to the far end of the tobacco field, Becky felt her heart sink, and perspiration saturated her armpits. It was the part of the field that had butted against Mr. Ruthmeyer's property, which now belonged to Mr. Tobin.

When Clemont led Judge to the affected leaves, he just stood back and pointed as if the blight might be catchy. Judge walked closer and inspected the leaves and stalks of the plants. It was a horrible sight. A small patch of tobacco plants that were normally a rich yellow-green at this time of year were now a sickly gray color as if they were covered in soot. As soon as Judge touched his finger to them, they practically disintegrated, crumbling to the ground and leaving smudges on Judge's fingers.

"What is it, Daddy?" Becky asked. "You've seen this before, right?"

Judge scratched his chin and leaned closer to the leaves. The stalks looked like cigars that had been left out in the rain, and even some of the roots appeared to have pulled themselves almost completely out of the dirt, lying limply and coiled on top of the soil. The smell the plants gave off was the same kind of sickly smell a person had when burning a high fever.

There was the faint familiar smell of tobacco, but underneath it was a yellow, hot, sweet scent that shouldn't have been there. It made Becky queasy.

"I'm afraid I haven't seen this before," Judge said. "Clemont, get the boys over here. Pull out everything that has this fungus on it and burn it immediately. It doesn't look to have spread too far."

"Yes, sir," Clemont said before putting his index finger and thumb in his mouth and giving a whistle. Three other workers in the area came running.

"That's all it is, Becky. Sometimes it happens." Judge shrugged.

"But you've never seen anything like it before?" She swallowed hard.

"No. But that doesn't mean anything. We'll get rid of these here plants before there's any more damage. Just a couple of bushes won't hurt this year's crops."

Becky looked over her shoulder at the land that had been Mr. Ruthmeyer's just a few short days ago. It seemed like years. Why had she had to come to watch the fire and even see Mrs. Tobin sobbing over him? Why had she had to see that cruel and stoic Leelee? She had never given Mr. Ruthmeyer a thought while he was alive. Now all she could do was wish he weren't dead and was back in his house doing whatever he was always doing.

"Daddy, you don't think this has to do with Mr. Tobin stopping by, do you?" Becky asked.

"What are you talking about?" Judge asked while still inspecting the leaves of the dying plants.

"The other night at your party, when Mr. Tobin showed up. He said he would get us if we came near his property," Becky said.

"He did? When was this?" Judge stood and scratched the back of his neck. Becky could tell he was only half listening to her as he clenched and unclenched his jaw and squinted at the plants like they might give up a clue as to what was wrong.

"Don't you remember?"

"I've got to admit, darlin', your old daddy tied one on that night. There's a heap I don't recall. Just don't tell your mother." He winked at Becky.

"I'm no stoolie." Becky tried to grin, but the corners of her mouth felt heavy.

She didn't see any point in pestering her father about Mr. Tobin any more. Besides, there was nothing to say this wasn't just some freak coincidence. Maybe the plants did just get some cootie they'd not seen before.

She had just started to walk back to the house

ahead of Judge when something caught her eye. The sun had glinted off something just a few short steps from where they were standing. Upon closer inspection, Becky saw it was a mason jar filled with dirt and seashells and bits of glass and rope. There was no question who had put this here. Becky also had no doubt that even if they burned the leaves that were affected, it wouldn't be the last they saw of this fungus on the plants. It very well might wipe out the entire crop.

Her first instinct was to tip over the jar, empty all its contents, and let the wind carry the debris where it may. But her gut told her otherwise. She would leave it alone and ask Cecelia tomorrow night at midnight. Why she had to wait, Becky didn't know. But it felt like it was going to take three days for the next twenty-four hours to go by.

Becky left her father dealing with the tobacco and the field hands. She'd just be in the way. Without thinking, she changed direction, skirted the house altogether, and snuck like a prairie dog through the stalks of tobacco toward the cemetery. She wanted to be alone to think.

That was no ordinary fungus. It wasn't just a couple of sick plants. It wasn't a disease that would be ended by tearing the plants up by the roots and burning them. That Leelee was dancing around in the shadows, and she had done this. Mr. Tobin was part of it. He wouldn't be happy until he wrecked everyone he thought had done him wrong, whether it was true or not.

CHAPTER TWENTY-ONE

The cemetery felt heavy, as if it was tired of being there. Becky walked from one end to the other. Part of her hoped maybe Adam was waiting on the other side near the entrance. But the entire area was empty as usual. That was just as well. What would she tell him? That she had brought a hex down on her family, and if she didn't do something, the crops Judge had nurtured his whole life would shrivel up along with everything else?

How am I ever going to fix this?

She finally took a seat underneath a moss-covered tree. It was cooler there. The air was rich with the moist smell of the foliage that sprouted all around her. The grass was cool, and as Becky looked at the ground, she saw ants marching about their business and heard the sweet melodies of the birds above in the branches.

After a few minutes, a visitor did come to see Becky. It was the little girl who had been crying when Leelee was digging up the graves of her friends. Her disposition had not changed.

"Hello, honey," Becky said.

"Hello," she replied. "I didn't think you were coming back."

"I almost didn't." Becky pulled her lips down at the corners. "I'm afraid I haven't figured out a way to help our friends."

"I miss them," the little girl said. "Especially Grandpa Wilcox."

Becky's heart lodged in her throat. She didn't dare think of the image she had seen of Mr. Wilcox on the Tobin property, crying out in frustration. Even those waiting to be called home should be left to do so in peace.

"What would you do if you were me?" Becky asked. "Maybe together we can come up with something."

The little girl pinched her eyebrows together and thought hard for a few minutes.

"If I could, I'd tell that lady to go away and never come back. And if she didn't listen to me, I'd get my pa to come and tell her so. She'd not dare go against him. He's big and strong. I once saw him lift a bag of corn on each shoulder and carry it to our wagon."

"Golly. He sounds strong," Becky replied.

"Yes, ma'am. I'd get him to stop her. But I'm not sure if I'll see him." She went back to thinking hard. "We just need to find someone bigger than her."

Becky smiled. Leelee was tiny. It would be hard to find someone who wasn't bigger than her. Her size wasn't the issue. It was her power. The only people Becky could think of who might even come close to being equal to Leelee were Cecelia and Ophelia, and they had already said they weren't able to go up against hoodoo.

"Lady?" The little girl looked up at Becky.

"Yes, honey?"

"Why do you glow so bright?"

Becky sat up straight and smiled. "I didn't know I did."

"You do. That's how I always know you are here." She grinned. "That's how my friends know you are here, too. You glow brighter than all of us."

"Do you glow, too? Because you don't look like a glow worm to me. You look just like a little girl," Becky replied, happy to be having a playful conversation.

"We all do. That's why the bad lady takes the dirt from the graves. It's where our glow is." The little girl looked off in the distance and then back at Becky before she smiled and faded away.

Becky sat there for a few minutes longer until her head started to hurt. Something that little girl had said was tickling the inside of Becky's head like a clue she couldn't see yet.

Her pa was big enough to stop Leelee, the little girl had said. Becky needed to find someone bigger than Leelee. Of course she did. That would be berries if she could find someone to bully her. That old Trotsky needed her clock cleaned.

"I'm running in circles," she said as she stood up and headed back to the house.

As soon as her home was in view, Becky saw Fanny on the porch. The sight of her annoying cousin ruffled Becky's feathers so much she didn't know if she wanted to laugh or cry. She opted for the former.

"Oh, there she is." Fanny pointed.

Who was she talking to? Lucretia? Kitty?

Just then a tall, blond, familiar form appeared. Stephen Penbroke was paying a visit. Becky smoothed the front of her dress and patted her finger curls into place. She squared her shoulders and lifted her chin before waving half-heartedly.

"You're lucky, Stephen. Normally Becky comes out of those fields covered head to toe in dirt." Fanny turned to Becky. "I'm sure your mother will be pleased the hem of your dress isn't torn, wet, or stained." Fanny chuckled as she patted Stephen on the arm.

Stephen smiled but not at Fanny's comments. Without giving her another look, he came down the back porch step, thrust his hands into his pockets, and strolled up to her.

"So what's cookin'?" he asked.

"What are you doing here?" Becky asked.

"I came to see you. I thought that with your mother's permission, I might be able to take you for a long drive somewhere," Stephen replied.

"Today might not be a good day. My father's got some sick plants back there. They need to burn 'em before the fungus spreads to the other plants. But I'm sure Fanny would love to go." Becky looked at her cousin, who was sitting in one of the porch rocking chairs, her skirt pulled dangerously high as she pretended to read the latest issue of *McClure's*.

"Come on, Becky. Just you and me. A change is as

good as a rest, and you look like you need a change," Stephen said.

"I'm sorry, Stephen. I'm never the one to be a flat tire, but I'm not up for an adventure today. However…" Becky suddenly had an idea that required she turn on the charm. "Tomorrow night is a different story."

"Tomorrow night?" He looked down at her as if the sheer notion of her having him come calling at night was the scandal of the decade.

"Oh, come on. You've been around the block. I can't possibly be the first tomato to ask you to pick her up when the owls are out." Becky smirked. "Unless you aren't interested. I'm sure I can get Teddy to drive me."

"Where are we going?" Stephen asked, his hands still in his pockets as he leaned in dangerously close so Becky could whisper in his ear.

"An apothecary downtown," Becky breathed.

"Sounds like a real barn burner." Stephen leaned back and snickered.

"But don't pull up in front of the house," Becky said, bouncing on her toes. "I'll meet you at the road."

"This sounds like a shady deal."

"Are you in or not?" Becky asked with her hands on her hips.

"I'm in. But if you're not there, I'm going to come looking for you if I have to wake up Judge, Kitty, and everyone as far as Poole County."

"I'll be ready. Just don't be late."

Becky strolled into the house without giving Fanny a second look. She was glad Stephen had stopped by. She wasn't sure what she'd have told Teddy if she had to bother him for his flivver again. And she couldn't completely disregard how handsome Stephen looked. But she had much more important things on her mind, and it wasn't even ten o'clock in the morning yet.

Letting out a deep breath, she took a seat in the kitchen. Without asking, Lucretia put down a cup of hot black coffee and two pieces of toast.

"What's wrong with you, gal?" Lucretia asked.

"Oh, I'm just worried about Daddy's crops. That's all," Becky lied. What could she tell Lucretia? That she'd been out trespassing and now thought she had gotten a hex put on her by some hoodoo woman?

"Oh, don't you worry about that. Your daddy's got the greenest thumb of anyone in four counties. Whatever is the problem, it won't affect the crops. At least not enough to make a dent in his harvest,"

Lucretia said as she washed a few dishes in the deep sink.

"I hope you're right."

"You know what you need? You need to get your head cleared. And I don't mean at no juke joint or in that graveyard," Lucretia said. "Moxley's got to go into town for Miss Kitty. You're going with him."

"I don't know, Lucretia. Seems like whenever I go somewhere, trouble follows," Becky harrumphed before taking a sip of coffee.

"Well, I ain't saying trouble won't follow you. But you need to get out of this house. Go get your nails done. Do something that will make your mama happy. When we get stuck, it's best to look outside ourselves. Bring a little joy to someone else, and you'll find it all comes back to you." Lucretia still hadn't turned around from her task.

"Maybe you're right." Becky stood after gulping down the last of the hot coffee.

"Lucretia, do you think you can stir up a pitcher of your sweet ambrosia?" Fanny asked as she sashayed into the kitchen as gracefully as a bull in a China shop.

"Yes, ma'am. I've got a bushel of limes," Lucretia said.

"I have the feeling we are going to have another

gentleman caller today. Becky, you might want to put on something more presentable," Fanny said. "I know Aunt Kitty has bought you nicer dresses than that one."

"I'm going to run an errand with Moxley. When's he leaving?" Becky asked Lucretia. "He's leaving soon, isn't he?"

"I think he's on his way to the car right now. In fact, you better run." Lucretia smirked with her back turned to Becky and Fanny.

"Good idea. Fanny, tell Mama I'll be back later." Becky dashed out the door and sure enough caught Moxley on the way to the coach house to get the car.

"But Becky, I think this person is coming to see you," Fanny huffed.

"Let her go," Lucretia said, chuckling. "She'll be back in plenty of time to reject whoever it is that's coming."

"Well, I just don't see why a girl with no prospects would want to turn down a male visitor," Fanny said.

"I'm sure you don't," Lucretia replied. "Ma'am."

"Just make the ambrosia," Fanny huffed before leaving the kitchen.

Once safely down the dirt road and far from the house and Fanny's comments, Becky let herself feel a little better. The sun was warm. Daddy's Renault drove smoothly. Moxley never had a lead foot, and today Becky didn't feel she was in a hurry to get anywhere or come back. She was happy feeling that in-between sensation of just being out in the world. While in the car, there was nothing she could do about the crops or Leelee or the jars of dirt that she left scattered around. Instead, she just listened to the sputter of the motor and let the miles go by.

"Miss Becky, how many times you think I saved you from your mama's matchmaking by taking you into town?" Moxley joked.

"Too many to count," Becky laughed.

"Your cousin Fanny certainly likes when gentlemen callers come to the door." He looked at Becky sideways.

"You noticed that too, huh?" Becky shook her head.

Moxley and Lucretia had never been merely employees to Becky. She loved them as much as any member of her family—and in Fanny's case, much more. The only problem was that it made it hard to hide anything from them. They were keen to pick up on Becky's emotions and at times were more in tune with her than her own mother was. Now was one of those times.

"I don't know why you feel the need to run away from that Cousin Fanny. She should be running away from you," Moxley continued. "That girl don't use the brains the good Lord gave her. If she did, she'd know not to be pressing her ear against the door every time someone starts a conversation she's not part of."

"You aren't just whistling Dixie, Moxley. I just don't know what Mama sees in her. So, where are we headed?" Becky chuckled.

Yup. If anyone saw what was going on around the house, it was Moxley and Lucretia. Fanny was a sneak. Her behavior made Becky regret ever coming to her defense when Hugh Loomis had been questioning her reputation. She doubted Fanny would ever do the same for her.

Moxley pondered out loud that he had a couple of projects that required a trip to the hardware store, and he was needing to pick up Mr. Mackenzie's suits from the seamstress.

"Drop me at the hen coop, Moxley. I think I'll take Lucretia's advice and get my nails done."

"Oh, that will be a wonderful treat," Moxley said even though Becky knew he thought getting her nails done was probably as wonderful as watching grass grow. "Don't take any wooden nickels. I'll be back for you in an hour."

As soon as Becky walked in, she realized that not only was she ready to converse with these old biddies, but they were happy to spill the beans about a treasure trove of things, including Mr. Tobin.

CHAPTER TWENTY-TWO

The beauty parlor in the middle of town had a double purpose. First and foremost, it was where the prominent ladies of Savannah compared notes on children and home life and shared valuable information on recipes, fashion, and the latest gossip in town. Secondly, it was a place where they could get their hair and nails done. When Becky walked in alone, not being dragged in by her mother, it was as if the ladies were seeing a ghost.

"Is that really Rebecca Mackenzie?" Helen-Lyn Merriweather gushed from her seat, where she was getting her hair pinned into tiny curls. She was quicker than the best scoop on a hot lead for the *Savannah Bulletin*.

"Hello, Mrs. Merriweather. Yes, it's me." Becky smiled politely.

If she did what she wanted, which was to march right up to the gossipy old hen and spit a raspberry in her face, she was sure the Women's Auxiliary would hand her mother a pink slip, banning her and any future generations from joining their prestigious organization. All the Women's Auxiliary amounted to was a traveling gossip column led by Mrs. Merriweather. She never missed an opportunity to tell Kitty Mackenzie she had seen Becky walking alone after nine o'clock or in a car with someone she didn't recognize from any of the finer families in town or wearing a dress that was not what she'd ever let *her* daughter wear.

The other women, following Mrs. Merriweather's lead, all chimed in, too. After a bit of small talk and telling the receptionist that she wanted her nails done the brightest red they had, Becky planted the seed.

"It was just terrible about Mr. Ruthmeyer. My daddy was there trying to help, but we were too late," Becky said. She didn't have to say anything else.

"I heard that he passed out drunk with a lit cigarette in his hand," Mrs. Pescolm confessed while stroking her long neck the way she did every time she offered up any information.

"I wouldn't be surprised," Mrs. Hannity interrupted and lifted all three of her chins. "I heard he was drinking more of that bathtub gin than he was selling and had started moving moonshine. My Dean won't go near the stuff. Says it's better suited to pour in the gas tank than down the gullet."

"I happen to know for a fact that Stella Tobin tried to run into the burning building to save him," Mrs. Merriweather said. She tilted her head back and looked down her arm all the way to her fingertips as she wiggled her fingers, making her jeweled ring flash brightly.

"Who told you that?" Mrs. Pescolm asked.

"Mrs. Rockdale. Her entire family was there trying to help. Why? I don't know. The man was strange. What Stella Tobin ever saw in him is a mystery to me," Mrs. Merriweather stated.

"Some women just have to do that," Mrs. Hannity added. "They aren't happy unless they are behaving no better than a dog in the street."

"Well, I heard that Mr. Ruthmeyer was dabbling in more than moonshine." Mrs. Sophia Russo jumped into the conversation with both feet.

Mrs. Russo was considered a stone's throw from

HARPER LIN

being a full-blown gypsy. The only thing that saved her from complete ostracism was the fact that she was very generous with her money at almost every charity event. Since she was both Italian and Catholic, it was a miracle any of the women spoke to her at all. But she was a billboard that wasn't afraid to advertise, and her sugar daddy, Mr. Russo, who owned a dry-cleaning business and was at least twenty years her senior, liked it that way.

"What did you hear, Sophia?" Mrs. Merriweather asked quickly.

Mrs. Russo looked around before leaning forward in her seat, where a quiet woman was silently painting her nails.

"I heard that he sign a contract with *spirito malign*. Evil spirit. That his fortune came from unsavory practices and a devotion to the Evil One." Mrs. Russo crossed herself as she said this. "He had strange idols around his house. If I had to guess, it looked like voodoo to me."

Becky gasped, coughed, then chuckled nervously. "Excuse me," she sheepishly said before nodding for Mrs. Russo to continue.

"Everyone knows that Mr. Tobin's maid is of a suspect religion. Those two, John and Earl, were thick as thieves before Stella came along." Mrs.

Hannity verified Mrs. Russo's suspicions. "Now, they've had a feud going on over three years. John claims Earl vandalized his property. Earl says John stole money from him. John says Earl can't be trusted and that his gin is no good. Earl says John is running a racket. Back and forth. Back and forth. And in between, a window would get broken here, a tire on a car would be slashed there. They lived to hate each other. It wasn't like either one couldn't have moved to another part of town. Nope. They had to stay neighbors."

"That had to be just awful for your family, Becky, being that Mr. Ruthmeyer's land ran right up to your daddy's fields," Mrs. Pescolm said, looking for more dirt.

"We never had a problem with Mr. Ruthmeyer. I can't say I ever saw the man but once in a while around town. Even then, he never said a word." Becky held her eyes steady and watched as the women quickly turned down her compassionate words for Mr. Ruthmeyer.

"It was the woman. She's the one who brought the poison between them," Mrs. Merriweather said as if she'd gotten it from high on a mountain. "And have you seen her around town lately? She glides down the street like Queen Sheba while she's delivering hooch to every dive in the city. What kind of a lady does that?"

"It's disgraceful," Mrs. Pescolm said.

"Obscene, if you ask me," Mrs. Hannity added. "Especially when everyone knows she was having an affair with John Ruthmeyer. She all but said so by showing up at his house, which her husband set on fire."

"Do you really think Mr. Tobin set the house on fire?" Becky asked.

They all stopped and looked at her as if she suddenly started singing in Chinese.

"Oh, Becky, don't be so naïve," Mrs. Merriweather snapped. "Of course he did."

"Then why haven't the police arrested him?" Becky continued prodding.

"The police have to have evidence." Mrs. Merriweather smirked.

"Yes, Becky, they can't just go around arresting people because they heard a rumor. My goodness, half of Savannah would be behind bars if that was the case," Mrs. Russo chuckled.

"But that means there is a murderer walking around," Becky replied.

"Well, maybe it wasn't Mr. Tobin who burnt down Mr. Ruthmeyer's house. Although who could blame him if Mr. Ruthmeyer and Mrs. Tobin were carrying on like I've heard they were?" Mrs. Merriweather said. "Mr. Tobin doesn't associate with the finer people of this town. I do believe he personally knows where several bodies are buried, and that keeps him well insulated. He probably has the cleanest hands out of the lot of them. I heard that he sells quite a bit of that white lightning to the clubs in those unsavory parts of town. You know what kind of people frequent those establishments."

Becky gaped. "What kind of people?"

No one answered. Becky knew the ladies thought she was flaky. She dressed differently from their prim-and-proper daughters. She wasn't shy about dancing with any gent who extended his hand. She had tied on an anchor more than once and had probably done so while unknowingly drinking Mr. Tobin's gin. And they knew she went from speakeasy to speakeasy every other night to do so. There would have been a collective pearl-clutching if Becky were to spill the beans and tell them all how many times she'd seen their proper daughters and sons at these establishments, acting chippy, cuddling in the dark corners, only to end up upchucking in the parking lot like some brush ape. Yes, these women thought they knew a lot about what went on in town but didn't have a clue what was going on right under their noses. Yet they seemed to love Fanny, who would steal their daughters' beaus without the slightest provocation and grin in their faces as she did so. The world was a strange place.

Suddenly, Mrs. Pescolm tossed out the new topic of Mr. R.H. Gavin taking ill.

"Ruth Gavin said he went out one day and came back with some kind of rash on him," she said. "They tried a dozen different remedies, but so far, nothing has worked."

"Now it's funny you should say that because I saw him fawning all over...I'll give you one guess," Mrs. Merriweather coaxed.

"Who? Who?" Becky thought the women all sounded like they pooped through feathers.

"Mrs. Stella Tobin. I saw him holding the door open for her, greeting her by her first name as if she were some kind of royalty," Mrs. Merriweather replied. "If he's ill, I know where he caught it."

The ladies whooped at Helen-Lyn's risqué innuendo.

"You don't think that Stella Tobin has moved on so quickly from Mr. Ruthmeyer, do you?" Mrs. Russo asked, practically salivating.

"I can't say. But I know that Mrs. Gavin has been

sleeping in the guest bedroom since he came down with his affliction." Mrs. Pescolm smirked.

Becky was torn between feeling disgust at the spinning yarns she was hearing and absolute terror at these same yarns. If Mr. Gavin were ill, if he had some kind of rash, it wasn't from anyone but Leelee, and she was punishing him for Earl Tobin. Just like she was punishing her father by ruining his tobacco.

It didn't take long for Becky to be quickly forgotten and all but ignored for the rest of her appointment. When her nails were dry, she stood up, told the old hens how wonderful it had been to see them, and exited the shop just as Moxley was pulling up.

"How was it?" Moxley asked.

"Like Daniel in the lion's den. But I got my nails done. Do you think Mama will like them?" Becky wiggled her fingers in front of her.

Moxley began to chuckle. "Miss Becky, I think she might find that shade of red to be a bit too much."

"Naw. She'll think it's ducky." Becky grinned.

With all the new information she had swirling in her head, Becky tried to sort things out on the ride back home. Martha might offer a chair to sit on that Becky hadn't considered. But she felt a shiver run over her shoulders as she thought of what Mrs. Russo had said.

"I heard that he sign a contract with spirito malign. *Evil spirit."*

Becky thought she was right.

CHAPTER TWENTY-THREE

The moon was full as Stephen drove Becky down the dirt road from her house toward downtown Savannah. His car purred, unlike Teddy's, which had the tendency to belch out a puff of black smoke every couple of miles and sometimes stuttered when it had to ride over gravel.

"It's on Bryn Mawr. Martha is supposed to meet us there." Becky drove from the passenger's side, telling Stephen which way to go.

"You didn't say anything about Martha coming along," Stephen said.

"Don't you like Martha? She's my very best friend. There isn't much I do without her." Becky lifted her chin.

"No, I think she's swell. A real live wire. But I

didn't think she'd come with her mother being ill and all," Stephen said casually.

Becky snapped her head in Stephen's direction. "Her mother is ill? How do you know? When did you hear this?"

"Well, I had run into Teddy when I was given the bum's rush at your place yesterday. He was on his way up to the Bourdeaux estate with an armful of flowers and a parcel of Bulgarian herb tea. I asked if he'd cheesed off Martha and was trying to mend some fences. He said it was for Mrs. Bourdeaux. Said the doctor had been to their house the morning after your parents' party and told Martha and her father that she had symptoms of typhoid fever. I thought you knew already; otherwise I would have high-tailed it back over to your side of the fence with the news."

"Typhoid fever?" Becky gulped. There was no way Mrs. Bourdeaux had typhoid fever. "Are you sure he wasn't pulling your leg? Teddy can have a strange sense of humor at times. Have you seen how he dresses?"

"I don't think he was fooling." Stephen pinched his eyebrows together.

Becky felt her eyes start to burn. The last thing she wanted was for Stephen to see her crying, but her bottom lip began to tremble, too. If he were to look at her, he'd see. Instead, Becky looked down and began to fuss with the hem of her skirt.

Stephen could sense something was wrong. It didn't take a genius to figure out that when Becky Mackenzie dummied up, there was a problem.

"I'm sure she'll be okay." He tried to soothe her as he drove.

"It's my fault," Becky whispered.

"Of course it isn't. Look, from what I hear, Mrs. Bourdeaux is tough as nails. Just because a sawbones tells you one thing, that doesn't make it so. And wouldn't Martha have contacted you by now had she really been worried?" Stephen asked.

"I suppose so."

"Well, she's your best friend. I can't imagine her not wanting your shoulder to lean on at a time like this. That's what makes me think it ain't worth worrying about just yet." Stephen raised his chin and smirked. Had it been any other day and any other time, Becky would have agreed and put the worry out of her mind. But this made three catastrophes in less than a week since she'd gone onto the Tobin property. All people she knew and loved.

What was she even going to see Cecelia for? She should have Stephen turn the car around right now and go rattle the rafters at the Bourdeaux house. Cecelia had all but said that there was nothing she could do. Hoodoo was a type of witchcraft she knew nothing about and didn't want to go anywhere near.

Poole County was in the opposite direction. Martha's family was behind them. Becky slumped in the seat and shook her head as her thoughts tumbled and tripped all over themselves. Nothing was clear.

"Are you all right, Becky?" Stephen asked.

"I'm fine. The place is on Bryn Mawr. You have to take a right up ahead, and then at the place that says Pete's Sliced Bacon, you take a left and…" Becky stuttered, not even hearing her own words until Stephen interrupted her.

"I know where we're going," he replied. "You forget, I lived here my entire childhood."

"Oh, that's right. I'm sure at the age of nine, you were swanning down the city sidewalks, looking for your blue serge," Becky snapped.

"I didn't have a sweetie at the age of nine. I told you I was waiting on you. No one else would do," he said in a singsongy tone.

"I wouldn't have pegged you as a wind sucker. But the more I get to know you, Stephen Penbroke, the more I think Fanny is your type."

Becky patted her hair into place as she blinked

back her tears. There was no use waking up the neighborhood just to tell Martha they were cursed. Martha probably already knew, and that was why she hadn't contacted Becky. She was mad at her. Why shouldn't she be? It was all her fault.

"Don't be daffy." Stephen shook his head, chuckling. "You're the monkey's eyebrows, and I don't plan on taking no for an answer. Let's just remember who showed up to take you on this wild-goose chase to some mysterious apothecary in the middle of the night."

Becky crossed her arms. He had a point. But she knew that if she'd seen Adam first, he'd have taken her to the moon if she asked him. Still, it was nice having Stephen along to keep her from being too nervous. She had no idea what Cecelia had in mind or why she had to show up at midnight. But after looking at her watch, she was afraid they were going to be late.

"Hey, let's drop the lead on that accelerator. We don't have much time."

"Your wish is my command."

And they flew into the busy nightlife, only to come to a screeching halt at 784½ Bryn Mawr.

"You wait here," Becky ordered before hopping

out of the car and dashing into the store without looking back.

"What?" Stephen barked, looking put out.

"It will only take me a minute. I'll be right back, and then we can head home,"

"Go home? Oh, no way, sister. You and I have some unfinished business."

"No we don't," Becky said as she slammed the door shut.

"Yes we do. And if you don't come with me to dip the bill, I might just have to tell your lovely mother and father what you're up to. And I'll do it in front of Fanny."

Becky could tell by the twinkle in Stephen's eyes that he was dead serious.

"That's blackmail."

"That's irrelevant. Will I need to come get you, or can I trust you won't sneak out the back way?" Stephen rested his right arm over the steering wheel and winked at her. He was good-looking and a real charmer. But Becky didn't like being painted into a corner.

"I won't sneak. But this ain't over, buster." She turned and was instantly reminded that there weren't just three victims of Leelee's wrath. Cecelia and Ophelia were the fourth and fifth.

The front window of the shop had been boarded shut, and there was a plank of plywood where the glass on the door used to be. A cardboard sign reading Open For Business dangled from a string around the doorknob. Becky felt a wave of embarrassment that she was the cause of the damage. Inside, the broken windows didn't seem to deter the customers; a shady group of night crawlers wandered up and down the aisles, looking for the cure to whatever ailed them.

Ophelia let out a loud whistle to catch Becky's eye. She jerked her thumb toward the stairs without saying a word. Becky nodded and hurried in the direction of the upstairs apartment. She'd gotten used to slipping past the small votive candles and the deceased relatives that were positioned around the stairwell and inside the apartment.

Everyone was easy to maneuver around except for Cousin Mimi, who was still mean even in the afterlife. She hissed at Becky as she walked past. Becky knew better than to roll her eyes or stick out her tongue at the rude woman. The last time she had done so, the feisty ghost had nearly thrown her down the stairs. Instead, she focused on the steps, hurried to the top floor, and knocked on Cecelia's apartment door.

"Come in! Quickly!" Cecelia called.

Within seconds, Becky was in the apartment and at her side. Cecelia was standing at the small table in front of the windows that led to the fire escape. The moon was in perfect view and shined its full white face at them. She took a large red medallion from around her neck, whispered some words that Becky didn't understand, then dropped it into a cup filled with tea.

"Drink this." She picked up the delicate cup and handed it to Becky.

"What is it?"

"It's arsenic. Now hurry up. We've only got a couple of minutes to get this right," Cecelia replied. "That's your problem. You ask too many questions. You want to know too much. Well, now you're going to know all you want to. Sit."

Cecelia pulled out the chair on the far side of the table and urged Becky into it.

"I'm sitting." Becky coughed as she swallowed the last gulp of tea. "This tastes like licorice. What's in it?"

"Wart of a frog. Spider eggs. A sliver of tombstone," she said seriously before starting to chuckle. "It's made with anise and fennel. Now shush."

Cecelia sat down across from Becky and pulled

out a small book. It looked old, and the spine was cracked from use. After opening it up to a page marked with a red velvet ribbon, she began to read. At first, Becky thought the words sounded like Latin, but other parts made her think maybe it was Gaelic. Her head began to swim a little, as if she was drunk, only without the queasiness or dizzy spells or feeling that her tongue had become too big for her mouth.

Then Cecelia took the medallion out of the teacup and placed it on a blue silk scarf. She folded the scarf over it, took Becky's hand, and placed it in her palm. In her other hand, she grasped a mason jar of dirt just like the ones Becky had seen at the Tobin place.

"What are you doing with that? What is it? I don't want it," Becky said fearfully, trying to pull her hands away.

"It isn't what you think. This is from the Ruth-meyer property. It holds the essence of what happened there," Cecelia soothed. "You have to trust me. Give me your other hand, Becky. We don't have a lot of time left."

Becky swallowed hard and reluctantly put out her other hand. Cecelia dumped the dirt into it. All of a sudden, Becky was on the Ruthmeyer property. She was in the house, and Mr. Ruthmeyer was there with Mr. Tobin. The men were smiling and talking while sitting on the floor.

"They're laughing like they are friends," Becky said as she watched the scene unfold in front of her like a movie. "They're sitting in a room with a couple of washtubs in it. And it looks like…they're making bathtub gin." Becky smiled. "Well, I'll be a monkey's uncle! I've drunk that gin! I recognize the label!"

Then Becky saw the two men sitting at a table in what looked like a kitchen. They were counting money—stacks of it. The bootlegging business had been going well from the looks of it. The men talked civilly to each other. There was no sign of anger or even a slight difference of opinion. But in the background was a shadow that floated back and forth. It wasn't just a dark form; it was Leelee. She was watching them as she went about her chores like a gator that barely peeked above the water to let its prey get good and comfortable before attacking.

"They were friends. It looks like they were good friends. Golly. What could have happened?" Becky muttered. Then she saw it—Mrs. Tobin. Only she hadn't been Mrs. Tobin at the time. She was Miss Stella Heade.

"I should have known. It was a woman that came between the men," Becky said out loud.

She was right that it was a woman, but it wasn't Stella Heade. It was Leelee. The hoodoo witch watched Miss Stella Heade pay more attention to Mr. Ruthmeyer than she did to Mr. Tobin. She didn't like that.

"Why? What business was it of hers if Stella liked Mr. Ruthmeyer more?" Becky asked but got no answer.

It wasn't long after Stella came along that Leelee was whispering in Mr. Tobin's ear things that weren't just gossip. They were worms of jealousy and hate, and they ate at Mr. Tobin's mind.

"You need her," Leelee hissed to Mr. Tobin. "You can't do this without her."

"She doesn't love me," Mr. Tobin said bitterly. "She loves John. I know it. I can see it in the way she looks at him. In the sound of her voice."

"Then give everything to Ruthmeyer. You have wasted everything I've taught you. This was your business. I made sure of that. Do you really think you could have done all this without me? Do you think the coppers would have left you alone? Do you think your neighbors wouldn't have stolen your moonshine? Do you not believe in my magic?" She scowled as if she was daring him to contradict her.

"But Leelee, you taught him, too. You said we were

stronger together. The gin and the moonshine was just the beginning, you said." Mr. Tobin was like a child pleading with a teacher to not tell his parents he was being naughty in class.

"Don't you contradict me! Ain't I been the one to take care of you your whole life? Ain't I been the one to show you the magic and teach you the ways of my people? Now it's time for you to put everything I taught you to use." She sneered.

"I thought it was copasetic, Leelee. I really did," Mr. Tobin said.

"Fine. You leave me no choice. I'll make her come to you. Is that what you want?" Leelee's eyes were on fire as she spoke to Earl Tobin. "That is it, isn't it?"

"Yes," he croaked.

"Fine. She lives with her mama and sister, don't she? Her daddy been dead some time? Ain't no one else looking out for them," Leelee said, already knowing the answers.

Again, Earl nodded his sweaty, heavy head.

After that, something took hold of Mr. Tobin. He changed. It was as if those words Leelee had growled at him were a poison. Becky saw how he became not just pushy with Mr. Ruthmeyer, not just mean but cruel. It didn't take long before it was cruelty for sport.

"You'll marry me," Mr. Tobin said to Stella as Leelee

looked on with a sinister grin on her face. *"You'll marry me and say yes in front of him."*

"You'd better do as he says, Miss Stella. We know where your mama lives. You want your mama to live a long time, don't you? To be happy in her old age?" Leelee hissed. You'll make Earl happy, won't you? If you don't, your mama won't be on this earth much longer."

Mr. Tobin married Stella in a strange wedding that Leelee oversaw. It didn't look like a Christian wedding. It looked more like a sentencing. And in Mr. Ruthmeyer's home, he cried as he carved strange symbols into his house, on the walls and floors, and began collecting strange things in mason jars, too.

"They were friends, and Leelee split them up using Mrs. Tobin. Why?" Becky muttered. "Was it just to keep Earl Tobin happy? How could he be happy knowing his wife loved another man?"

Becky blinked as the images paraded past. Stella Tobin didn't let that strange ceremony keep her away from Mr. Ruthmeyer. They did have an affair. Becky saw them confess their love for one another. John Ruthmeyer held Stella in his arms, and she cried into his chest. It wasn't scandalous or sordid like the ladies at the hen coop had said. It was sad.

Then, like a glitch in the film, Becky suddenly

saw Mr. Ruthmeyer in his attic. He was unconscious. Smoke was filling up the room quickly.

"I don't want to see any more," Becky whispered, but it was as if no one heard her. Mr. Ruthmeyer's hair was matted to his head as he slowly began to come around. His shirt had become dark in the front, and when he sat up, the entire right side of his face was red with blood.

"I don't want to see any more, Cecelia! Oh, Mr. Ruthmeyer was hurt. He was hurt and left in the attic." Becky stared straight ahead as she watched Mr. Ruthmeyer crawl toward the door. It wouldn't open. He was trapped as the smoke became thicker and thicker.

A man stuffed a pack of matches into his pocket and then picked up a mason jar of clear liquid. He took a long, deep drink as he watched the Ruthmeyer house go up in flames. It wasn't Mr. Tobin. It was the man, Edward, who Becky had danced with at the Crazy Calico. That man had held her as tightly as he had Mr. Gavin while Leelee put that hex on him.

"I don't want to see any more, Cecelia!" Becky cried. "Edward was the one who set fire to Mr. Ruthmeyer's house! He locked him in the attic and left him! Mrs. Tobin was too late. She was running to help him, but she was too late!"

Becky saw the flames start to lick up the walls of the attic. The small window was his only hope. She heard her father's voice yelling for Mr. Ruthmeyer. He stumbled to the window, but his injury was too much. He couldn't stand. The flames were getting higher. The heat was unbearable.

"Cecelia! Make it stop! I don't want to see any more! Please! Make it stop!"

Becky cried as she stared ahead in horror, seeing Mr. Ruthmeyer cough and gasp as he tried to escape only to have the entire floor give way to the flames. Mr. Tobin told his wife her lover was dead. He smiled and laughed insanely as he told her as if even he couldn't believe it.

"And you and Leelee are my alibis. I've been here with you the entire time." He laughed. "No one would ever suspect Edward of anything. You could scream it from the rooftops, and no one would believe you. Just remember that. No one would believe you."

In a flash, Becky was back in Cecelia's apartment. Her whole body was trembling. When she opened her left hand, the features of the medallion wrapped in the blue scarf were imprinted in the meat of her palm. The moon was behind a patch of clouds, and the clock showed ten after midnight.

"I'm sorry you had to see all that, Becky." Cecelia took the medallion out of Becky's limp hand and set it on the table. "It was the only thing I could do that might give you a leg up on them. Was there anything that might help? Anything at all?"

It took Becky a few minutes to work up enough spit to swallow. Her mouth had gone bone-dry, and she felt like she'd just stepped out of a dark circus tent into the light. She looked at her right hand and the dirt that was now compressed into her palm.

"Mr. Ruthmeyer and Mr. Tobin were both involved with this hoodoo, but Leelee obviously preferred Earl Tobin over Mr. Ruthmeyer."

"He had to be the easier of the two to control," Cecelia said, nodding.

Becky told Cecelia what the moonshiners had done to Stella Tobin and why she had married Mr. Tobin. "She didn't love him, but they threatened her mother. Like they've done to me. They are going to get at me through my family and friends. Cecelia, I'm so sorry. I brought this right to your doorstep. And all I can say is…what now?" Becky whimpered.

"I don't know. But at least you know the story. And you know that Mr. Tobin doesn't get his hands dirty. Leelee does his bidding and gets other men to kill for him." Cecelia looked scared. "Maybe Mr. Tobin is the weak link."

In that split second, Becky thought of what Moxley had been saying about Fanny. The girl had everything done for her, arranged for her, provided for her because she was too dumb to know how to rub two nickels together. She was doted on because she couldn't survive any other way. Just like Earl Tobin.

"Mr. Tobin is the weak link. That's why he's never around doing any of the heavy lifting. Even Stella has to do the bootlegging to the speakeasies. He is incapable of handling anything. And he certainly couldn't be trusted to carry through setting the Ruthmeyer home on fire. That's why Edward did it," Becky said. "And it's Leelee who poisoned Daddy's crops and is making Martha's mother and Mr. Gavin sick. I'll bet my last dollar it was Edward who did in your storefront window, too. Mr. Tobin was nowhere around."

"Becky, didn't Ernesto see you the other night?" Cecelia asked.

"Of course he did. He told me to come here tonight," she snapped, annoyed that Cecelia wasn't following her train of thought.

"Where is the juju bag I gave you?" Cecelia asked.

"The what?"

"Ernesto was supposed to give you a juju bag to wear. I told him to tell you to keep it around your neck at all times." It was Cecelia's turn to sound sharp.

"Oh, that! I gave it to Martha. I hoped it would help keep her safe. I guess it kept her safe but not her mother."

"What do you mean?" Cecelia asked.

Becky told her what she heard about Mrs. Bourdeaux and what was happening to Mr. Gavin.

"Then there are Daddy's crops and your windows. The circle around me just keeps getting wider."

"Becky, that juju bag was to protect you. To keep you hidden." Cecelia shook her head. "It was all I could do. You'd been wearing disguises when you stumbled on their moonshine still. You might have been able to tell them that the 'boys' who went onto their property were a couple of bindle stiffs your daddy had hired and that they hopped the rails for parts unknown."

Becky stared at Cecelia and shook her head. "I can't seem to do anything right."

"I should have delivered it myself. Then you

would have known how important it was. I should have known you'd give it away to protect someone else. That's part of your glow, Becky."

At the word *glow*, Becky chewed her bottom lip for a few seconds before she leaned back in her chair.

"Cecelia, you got all that wallop from that little bit of dirt from Mr. Ruthmeyer's land?"

"I got the dirt. *You* brought out the wallop." Cecelia grinned.

"I've got an idea. It's a long shot. But I've got to try." Becky stood up and went to the door.

"What are you going to do?"

"I might just have to make a deal with the devil." Becky sighed.

Before Cecelia could say another word, Becky was out the door and heading down the stairs. When she reached the store, she found Stephen inside, staring into a glass case of exotic roots and herbs.

"Come on," she said, slipping past Ophelia and grabbing him by the hand.

"What kind of a store is this?" he gasped as he stood, still pointing to the strange objects in the case.

"It's a specialty shop," Becky replied.

"Who shops at a place like this?" he whispered.

"People who need…dried scorzonera root," she replied. "Now come on."

"What is dried scorzonera used for?" Stephen continued to fuss.

"I think it's used to shut the mouths of annoying men who won't leave when they are asked," Becky panted. "Don't worry about that now. Bye, Ophelia!" She waved and pulled Stephen out the door.

"That old lady had one gray eye." Stephen shuddered.

"I know. I think she can see ghosts with it," Becky replied.

"That gives me the heebie-jeebies."

If that scared him, Becky was sure she couldn't take him where she planned to go next.

He tried to put her on trial the whole way back. One question led to another and another. By the time they got to the long dirt road that led to her house, Becky was looking forward to her gruesome task as long as it meant there was some quiet.

Before Stephen got too curious, Becky informed him that she thought she, Ophelia, and Cecelia might have a cure for what was eating her father's tobacco. It bothered her that she could lie so easily, but it was necessary. If Stephen knew the truth, he certainly wouldn't believe it, and if he mentioned it to his family, they'd most definitely be chirping in Kitty's ear by the time the sun came up. She asked him to stop the car where he'd picked her up and made him promise not to tell anyone where they'd gone or to follow her.

"Why don't you want me to tell anyone where we were?" Stephen asked, again with the questions.

"I just don't think it's anyone's business," Becky replied.

"We went to a drugstore, where I waited for you for fifteen minutes, and when I went inside, some creepy old dame with a white eye gave me a once-over before you rescued me. That sounds like a program for the radio if I ever heard of one."

"Look, I don't have all night to explain proper manners to you. I'm asking you to keep it mum," Becky huffed. "I'm sorry if the evening didn't turn out as you'd hoped."

"Don't be daffy. The evening isn't over yet. It's still early. I know you know half a dozen dives that still have their lights on. Come on. Let's go for one spin somewhere."

"That sounds swell," she replied as she hopped out of the passenger's seat. "But not tonight. You're a swell egg, Stephen. Really you are."

"Wait. Is that it?" He hopped out from behind the

steering wheel and stopped Becky in her tracks. "I drove all the way down here to show you a good time."

"I had a good time. No. A great time. And now time is up. Good night, Stephen."

Becky waved and had started the long walk toward her house when Stephen took her hand and held her fast.

"I don't know what it is about you, Rebecca Mackenzie, but you've got me in knots." Stephen smiled devilishly.

"It's probably just indigestion," she said as she hurried away from him and toward her house.

When she heard the engine start again, Becky quickly darted into the tobacco field and headed toward what was left of Mr. Ruthmeyer's home. If she'd just waited a few more minutes, Stephen wouldn't have seen her and decided to follow at a distance.

CHAPTER TWENTY-FOUR

There was a jumble of puzzle pieces in Becky's head. As she huffed through the tobacco plants, smelling their sweet scent and feeling their cool, smooth leaves against her skin, she tried to calm herself and fit the pieces together.

The dirt from Mr. Ruthmeyer's property had something strong in it. Becky had seen exactly where the firefighters had laid Mr. Ruthmeyer's body when they removed it. There had to be some kind of value in that. If she could get Leelee to trade —Martha's mother and her father's crops for the magic in that dirt—maybe, maybe she could save them.

"She's not going to make it that easy," Becky muttered as she reached the fence that separated the

Mackenzie property from Mr. Ruthmeyer's. When the moon wasn't behind a patch of clouds, it gave off enough light for Becky to see where she was going.

"This is crazy," she continued. "I don't know what I'm doing. This is as creepy as Leelee digging in the cemetery."

Her legs ached from wearing the wrong shoes to walk the field in. She tried to distract herself from the gruesome task at hand. But when she looked at the remains of the house, she saw more than just the shell of a home. A faint glow hovered where they had laid Mr. Ruthmeyer's remains. There had to be some kind of essence of the man left there—something Leelee wouldn't know about, or else she would have had her goons with the sewn-up lips harvest the dirt for its power by now.

"I'm sorry, Mr. Ruthmeyer. I'm sorry this happened to you. But if you could see your way clear to help me, maybe you'll get to see Stella again, just for a minute," Becky said as kindly as she could.

There might have been bits of his burnt skin mixed with the dirt. If it was powerful enough for her to see the story behind Mr. Ruthmeyer's murder, then it might be strong enough to bargain with. Maybe.

With nothing but the pockets of her skirt to carry

the dirt in, Becky headed off in the direction of the Tobin house. The light kept waning every few minutes as clouds silently floated across the sky. Stars played hide-and-seek with her as she looked up into the darkness. It was beautiful and haunting at the same time. Becky could feel at one with the nature all around her and at other times feel like a stranger trespassing.

"If that isn't spot-on, I'll be a monkey's uncle," she muttered again.

Finally, she saw the Tobin house up on the hill. Her feet burned with blisters, and she knew her stockings were shredded beyond repair.

Suddenly, the scent of moss and bark was replaced by the smell of smoke. Something was burning. Becky was trying to guess which direction it was coming from when she spied a flickering bit of orange color in the distance. It wasn't the Tobin house on fire or any other house, but it was a fire burning. As Becky carefully and quietly felt her way toward the glowing light, she heard voices.

They were too far away for her to make out what they were saying, but they were chuckling and rambling as if something very exciting was going on. For some reason, Becky felt the need to pat the dirt in her pockets. It brought her a small sense of relief even though she had no idea if her plan was going to work.

It didn't matter. She'd give Leelee whatever she wanted if she promised not to hurt her father or Mrs. Bourdeaux. The thought made her feet feel as if they were weighted with chains. What was she doing? What would happen if the woman just stepped aside and played dumb about all of it?

You know darn well what will happen. Daddy's crops will blow away on the wind, and so will Martha's mother. And it will be your fault. That was the part that stung the most.

The glowing fire became bigger, and Becky soon realized it was a simple bonfire on the edge of the Tobin property, just a hop, skip, and jump from the moonshine still. Those men she heard were obviously imbibing in a late-night nip. Becky envied them that. She would have loved a champagne cocktail at the moment.

"So now what are you going to do?" she asked the darkness.

Just then, there was a rustling behind her. She froze, her hands instinctively going to her dirt-filled pockets to prevent any of Mr. Ruthmeyer from spilling out.

The sounds of leaves rustling and something

grunting and huffing made her think a herd of deer might have been passing. Those creatures got ornery at night, cavorting away from human eyes.

Her shoes made her wince each time she took a step, but Becky continued toward the house. Her skirt snagged on a sticker bush, making her gasp when she thought someone had caught hold of her. But as she yanked it free, hearing the fabric tear, she sighed. Another dress ruined.

Just walk right up there, Becky. Don't think about being terrified. Just walk up there and tell them what you've got. It doesn't matter if that old witch wants it or not. She'll want something from you, and by golly, you'll give it to her, because this whole mess is your fault. Now, take your medicine.

Her pep talk helped for about ten seconds as she emerged from the woods at the edge of the circle of light from the fire. That was when her best-laid plan blew up in her face.

"What are you doing here?" she said.

"I was following you." Stephen was standing in front of Edward, who had the double barrels of a shotgun jammed into Stephen's kidney.

"Who asked you to?" Becky clenched her hands into fists. "That man's going to fill you full of daylight, all because you had to see where I was going."

"Who walks off into a tobacco field at one in the morning?" Stephen argued.

"Someone who lives on a tobacco farm!" Becky snapped.

"Oh, that's just ducky. Look, pal, you don't need to hold that piece on me. Now that I found her, we'll be going," Stephen said. Edward smirked and jerked the shotgun back before plowing it into Stephen's side and knocking him to the ground.

"Break it up!" Becky yelled. "He's small potatoes. I think your boss is more interested in me. Why don't you get her down here so I can talk business."

"Why don't you drop that rod and fight me like a man." Stephen coughed as he struggled to his knees.

"You can't reason with this guy, Stephen. He only takes orders from a woman. He burned down Mr. Ruthmeyer's farm for her. He won't hesitate to fill you full of buckshot as well. Isn't that right, Edward?"

Edward's face fell as he stared at Becky. He might as well have just asked how she knew he committed the murder the way his jaw started working.

Stephen looked up at the man and then down again at his hands, which were splayed in front of him. He was also obviously trying to come up with a plan to save them both. But little did Stephen know that even if they did manage to get away, they wouldn't be free. Not by a long shot.

"Where's your boss? I don't have all night," Becky yelled.

"Mr. Tobin will be right back," Edward snarled.

"Ha! Mr. Tobin? He's not your boss! I'm talking about the woman with the scarf on her head. Leelee."

Edward was getting more and more upset every time Becky spoke.

"Either you go get her for me, or I'll just start calling for her myself."

Everyone stood still. The only movement came from the fire. The light danced off the trees and made the shadows come to life like tall, thin creatures hopping from place to place. The orange glow made the darkness look even more consuming than when Becky had been in it.

"Edward, what's going on out here?" It was Earl Tobin. He came stomping out of the house and marched right up to them.

"Looks like we've got some trespassers," Edward said gleefully.

Mr. Tobin stood in between Becky and poor Stephen, who was still on the ground, and started to

269

laugh. "Trespassers? Why, we'd be within our rights to shoot both of you. And I think that might be just what we..." His sadistic smile quickly folded into a frown as he looked more closely at Becky.

"I need to talk to your boss." Becky cursed her voice for trembling.

Mr. Tobin wasn't who she was really afraid of. But as he stood there staring at her, the memory of seeing her at Daddy's party as plain as the nose on his face, Becky feared she would not only not get the spell off her daddy's crops but also might not see the sun rise.

"I knew it was you. I told her that it weren't no boy that was spying in our woods," Mr. Tobin hissed. "I could tell by the way you run away that you and your accomplice were girls. Men don't run with their elbows flying in all directions."

"You did say that, Earl," Edward concurred.

"Well, that's a mighty brilliant deduction on your part. You're a regular scholar. Now, if you don't mind, I said I want to talk to your boss."

Becky didn't know why she used those words. They tumbled out of her mouth like men making a prison break. There was no way to stop them.

Mr. Tobin glared at Becky and pinched his lips together.

"You do know she's the big cheese, don't you? You're not the one running the racket on your own land. She is." Becky shrugged as if what she was saying was the most common, casual fact in the world. "Now get her."

Mr. Tobin walked up to Becky and stood toe-to-toe with her. He looked down at least six inches and smelled foul. But it wasn't just the smell of a man who had worked a field. It was a sickly smell that came from the inside, as if something had gone off and had yet to be thrown away. His clothes were dirty, stained with sweat and grime. This was not a man who was reaping the ill-gotten gains of his long-time enemy. This was a man who was ill.

"I think you need to watch your mouth, little girl. Your daddy ain't here to save you. That witch in town ain't here to save you. That Bruno on the ground ain't going to save you. The way I see it, you're behind the eight ball."

"You can see it any way you want. I don't care what you do. You're just the lackey. I said I wanted to talk to the big shot running this operation. I'm sure she knows I'm here." Becky was starting to get annoyed. If she was going to give up her eternal soul to save her father and her friend, she wanted to move things along.

Just then, the fire started to grow as if someone had doused it with a splash of gasoline. The flames licked high and snapped their long orange fingers up into the air before simmering. The wood crackled and popped, sending little red sparks off in all directions. The bonfire and the full moon made Becky suddenly realize this was probably the worst night on the calendar to face a hoodoo witch.

"Are you looking for me?" The same gravelly voice Becky had heard when she was underneath the window came from behind her.

She whirled around to find herself almost nose to nose with the woman with the scarf around her head. Leelee. She had a strange smell about her, as if she spent all her time in a root cellar. And Becky couldn't help but notice the stringy but strong muscles that showed on her arms and up her neck.

Becky stepped back a few paces with her hands raised. "Yes," she stuttered.

"Well, here I am. You are the one who has been on my property," she said.

"Is it *your* property? I thought this was Mr. Tobin's property. I guess if he's working for you, it is yours." Becky told herself to try and stop being sarcastic. It never helped her situation do anything but get worse.

"State your business, girl." Leelee's breath was hot and foul. She had a rotting cemetery of teeth in her mouth, and she continually worked her jaw like a cow chewing its cud. Her eyes looked red in the fire.

"You're right. I'm the one that's been on your property. You put something in my family's tobacco fields. I want you to take it away." Becky didn't sound brave or convincing. In fact, she thought her speech sounded downright pitiful. "And the sickness at the Bourdeaux place. That too."

"Ha ha," Leelee hissed. Behind her, from the small shed with all the strange jars and statues and etchings, came a desperate clatter. "Do you remember my friends? From the cemetery?"

Becky had forgotten about the men with their mouths sewn shut. How could she have just put that out of her mind and forgotten about it?

"They've been missing you. I told them to be patient and that you'd be joining them soon. Trespassers. That's what they were." Leelee smiled happily. "Coming to steal my moonshine back when I first got started in New Orleans. When Earl was just a baby."

"That's impossible. They'd be old. Those men wouldn't be able to run or...dig or..." Becky muttered.

"Ha ha ha! You see how much you don't understand! Ah…but it's too late. You and your friend are too late." Leelee smiled innocently.

"You just hold your horses. If anyone was trespassing, it was you," Becky said. "I caught you in my cemetery, digging up the graves of those people who were waiting to cross over. You were trespassing, and you were taking what I was there to protect. Now, I've come to make you a right fair offer."

"Little girl, you really think you have anything I want?"

"I have the dirt where Mr. Ruthmeyer was laid after they found his body. You think I don't have a clue as to what you're taking my cemetery ground for? I know what it holds. That essence is stronger than that moonshine for you."

Becky felt disgusted as she watched Leelee's eyes become wide with desire.

"You're lying."

"No. I was there with my father. I heard Mr. Ruthmeyer screaming before Mrs. Tobin came running. I saw where they laid his remains. And I have that in my pockets." Becky watched Leelee lick her lips. "But you have to do something for me."

"Ha. You want me to restore your tobacco fields.

Remove the decay that will consume the whole plantation within ten days. Is that it?" Leelee smirked.

"And Martha Bourdeaux's mother. She's ill. They had nothing to do with my trespassing. I dragged Martha along. She's got no idea about what's going on." Becky took a deep breath. "If you do those two things, I'll give you this dirt."

Leelee looked Becky up and down. Becky didn't know it, but Leelee could see her glow just like the little girl at the Old Brick Cemetery could. She envied it.

"I'll do it," Leelee finally replied.

"Leelee, that's not what you said," Mr. Tobin protested. "We can't just let these two go. Not for the blood soil of a thousand men. We can't do it. You said we'd wipe them out. Drive them crazy with despair. That was what you promised."

"Hush, boy," Leelee said, never taking her eyes off Becky. "Let me see it."

Becky reached deep inside her pockets and carefully scooped out the dirt she'd collected. But before she could do anything else, a voice rang out. "STOP!"

Leelee whirled around and hissed. Her hands shot up like cat claws ready to swipe, and her shoulders hunched up to her ears. Becky followed the sound of the voice and saw Mrs. Stella Tobin standing on the porch. She looked like a rag doll that had been mercilessly tugged and tossed.

"Stella, this don't concern you," Mr. Tobin spat.

"It don't? You're talking about the man I love, and you say it don't concern me?" She laughed bitterly.

In the firelight, Becky could see that Stella's cheeks were wet with tears. Quickly, Becky slipped the dirt back into her pockets.

"I told you not to talk that way."

"You told me a lot of things, Earl. You told me that you'd leave John be if I came with you. But you let her make the decisions for you." Stella nodded toward Leelee. "All these years, I've been afraid of what you'd do to me. Don't you see? You can't do anything to me."

"If you don't get back in that house, I'll…"

"You'll what, Earl? Beat me? Lock me in my room? Make me deliver your hooch for you? Or should I say her hooch. Little girl, you're right. She is the big boss here. This ain't the home of no man. Just a *boy* who can't give up the *teat*."

Becky gasped and looked to Stephen, who was still on the ground as Edward continued to hold his shotgun on him. Edward was just staring at what was happening.

"That's it!" Earl Tobin shouted. His voice gave

away his embarrassment. He took two steps toward the porch then froze in his tracks.

"Don't you move." Stella raised a pistol in her hand and cocked the hammer like any gumshoe on the beat might. "None of you."

Becky held her breath. Now what was she going to do? She was caught with the ground Stella's lover had died on and was looking to make a trade to save her family and friends. It didn't look good. Had she been in Stella's place and had the dirt been the ground Adam had been laid on, how would she feel toward the person looking to make a swap? Not very favorably, to say the least. Becky felt she was no better than Leelee.

When she looked at the old hag, she caught her calculating something. The woman was up to no good as sure as Becky was standing there. Without thinking, Becky raised her hands high and marched up to Stella.

"I remember you," Stella said.

"This doesn't belong to them." Becky reached into her pockets and pulled out the dirt, placing it in a small pile at Stella's feet. "Maybe it's not right what I'm doing. My whole family will be ruined. My best friend's too. But we'll be together. This belongs to you. I'm sorry."

"No! That's mine!" Leelee grunted angrily. "You come here, gal! You get over here and…"

"Becky!" Stephen jumped up, only to get the butt of the rifle to the back of his head. He groaned and fell back to the ground with his eyes closed as he put his hand to his skull.

Suddenly, the air shifted. The fire began to shrink as the wind picked up. The doors to the shed began to shake violently, and Becky was afraid those two goons were going to break out and charge her any minute. From the woods, she could see lights approaching.

"No! This ain't possible!" Leelee shouted.

"What? What is it, Leelee?" Mr. Tobin cried nervously. He looked around and squinted into the woods, but he didn't see anything.

"You all get back! Get back!" Leelee shouted. "What did you do?" She whirled around at Becky, reached out, and wrapped her bony hands around her throat. Becky scratched at her arms, which were powerful for a woman her age and size. "You broke my jars! You broke my jars and let them go!"

"I didn't!"

Becky looked at the ghostly figures quickly approaching. Only Leelee and herself could see the spirits. There were dozens of them. And they were advancing. Edward was looking toward the woods, the barrel of the shotgun visibly shaking as he tried to see what Leelee was seeing. He let off one shot and then another and another, but he didn't hit anything.

"Stop shooting!" Mr. Tobin ordered. "There ain't nothing there. Leelee, what's the matter? I don't see anyone. Who's out there?"

"You broke my jars! You broke my jars!" Leelee stuttered with spit rolling out from between her rotted teeth and coating her chin.

"I didn't do it," Becky hissed as she twisted and tore herself from the woman's grasp. Becky stumbled to the ground, and before Leelee could pounce on her, Stella jumped from the porch and slapped the old woman across the face.

"I've been waiting three years to do that to you. I broke your jars. Your prisons!" Stella screamed through tears. "I broke nearly every one of them!"

"That's it. I'm going to kill you!" Leelee said, her voice wild and raspy.

"You?" Stella laughed loudly and from deep inside. "You won't lay a finger on me. Who will you have do it? Edward? If he can recover from wetting himself, maybe he'll have enough wherewithal to load the shotgun. But I don't think his nerves will be steady enough to hit the side of the house."

Edward didn't hear a word. He knew there were spirits around. Only that could make the hair stand up on the back of his neck. He dropped the shotgun and took off running into the woods. Becky watched as several ghostly specters gave chase.

"I've lived through worse than this. You think you can beat me? I have been protecting him for years." Leelee jerked her thumb at Mr. Tobin and smirked. "I am his only family. Sadly, Earl will become a widower tonight."

"Do you think I'm afraid to die?" Stella asked. "Do you think you can get Earl to do your dirty work? He's never done it before."

"He'll do as I say. Earl, take that shotgun and end this!" Leelee commanded.

By now the ghostly spirits were at the edge of the firelight. They were watching and waiting as if something had to happen before they could strike. What was it?

Mr. Tobin stood stone-still. "I'm not a murderer," he muttered. "I'm a small-time bootlegger at best. Even at that, all I did was stir the gin. I'm no better than any dandy on the street."

"Shoot her!" Leelee screamed.

"She's my wife," Mr. Tobin all but sobbed.

"She doesn't love you! Shoot her! Shoot her dead or I'll…"

The gun went off!

Becky looked down at herself, afraid maybe she'd gotten the worst of it and didn't notice. But there was no blood, no smoke. She looked to Stella, who was just a few feet from her. She was swaying, but she didn't have a mark on her either. Her face was frozen in shock.

Then Becky looked at Leelee. The bitter old hag clutched at her shoulder. Mr. Tobin had shot her. But as with everything he had tried to do on his own in life, he'd missed the mark. Blood ran down her arm, but Leelee emitted a shallow, vicious laugh.

"You're damned, boy!" she said, raising a knotted, bony finger and pointing it at him. "I curse you and the next generation and the next…"

"You can't do that, Leelee," Stella said sweetly. "There won't be any future generations of the Tobin family. The name dies with him."

Leelee screamed like the wounded animal she was. The blood continued to run from her wound. She wouldn't be able to stand on her feet much longer, let alone work any of her hoodoo. Stella's words were like a blow, knocking the woman to the ground.

The spirits that had been waiting, their faces silently shouting, all grinned and laughed at once as they slowly began to advance.

"No! No! Get back!" The old woman swatted with her one good arm as she tried to crawl away on her knees. But she didn't get far before she ran into Stella.

"Why, Leelee? Why did you have to kill him?" Stella asked.

Leelee's face, which had been contorted by fear and pain, shifted into a sadistic grin as she stared up at Stella.

"Because you loved him."

That was all Leelee said before the spirits gathered around her. Stella couldn't see them. Mr. Tobin, who had dropped the shotgun and was staring at his own hands as if they weren't even his, was also blind to the spirits. Stephen was slowly coming around but was unaware of what was going on around him.

Only Becky and Leelee could see the spirits. They crept forward as Leelee attempted to crawl toward the shed. She scratched and clawed at the dirt, her sinewy legs kicking behind her as she struggled to get away. But it was no use. She'd lost too much blood to focus. The pain from her wound made her head swim. And for the first time in a long time, Leelee was afraid. Terrified.

The first spirit reached her. It was a man in a respectable Confederate uniform and dashing goatee. He'd been laid to rest many, many years ago in the Old Brick Cemetery and was waiting to be called home. How dare this witch disturb his final resting place? He took hold of her limp, wounded arm and held her fast while he swung his other arm like an ax overhead and plunged it into her chest. It wasn't her heart he was after. He wasn't hurting her physically. He couldn't; he was just a spirit. But he could reach the one thing that was in her heart. Her soul resided there.

By this time, a few more of the souls she had disturbed had come to take their revenge.

The last thing Becky saw was Leelee's own glowing spirit being torn from her body, screaming and kicking as it faced the court of its peers before her final judgment.

It was too much, so Becky turned her attention to Stephen. She scrambled over to him, raising him slightly to look into his face. There was no blood on the back of his head, but a giant goose egg had developed that would be pounding away the Anvil Chorus by sunrise.

But before Becky could get his arm around her shoulder and pull him to his feet, Mr. Tobin came out of his shock. Perhaps it was Leelee's screaming—or the fact that it had suddenly stopped—that snapped him out of it. Becky froze, fearful he was going to grab the shotgun and finish a job for once in his life.

"What have I done?" he stuttered with tears in his eyes.

At first, Becky thought he was talking to Stella. She watched as his body began to shake and tears rolled freely down his face. Any second now, he would confess to her that he had been so wrong, had been so blind, and that he was sorry. He'd beg her forgiveness, and she would grant it. Or at least that's what Becky thought would happen. She couldn't have been more wrong.

CHAPTER TWENTY-FIVE

"**L**ook what you made me do!" Mr. Tobin cried to Stella as he pointed at Leelee's lifeless body.

Becky didn't dare move. She didn't even blink as her eyes bounced from Mr. Tobin to Stella to what was left of Leelee lying on the ground. To the naked eye, she had been shot and bled to death. But Becky could see the justice the ghosts had obtained as they dragged her spirit into the darkness.

"So kill me, Earl. I'm already dead to you on the inside. I've never loved you. If you kill me, I'll be with John. Do you think I'd be scared of that?" Stella stared and stood straight.

"You did love me! She said you would learn to.

Leelee said she'd make sure of it!" Mr. Tobin sobbed like a child.

Had he not had a shotgun at his feet, ready to use it at the slightest provocation, Becky would have slapped him across the face. She was embarrassed for him. There was no pity here. No compassion. All the fear he had instilled in people all over town had been just a mirage. Mr. Tobin wasn't even the schoolyard bully; he was the sidekick to the bully. And now that someone bigger and badder had taken care of that bully, Mr. Tobin was left all alone, unable to fend for himself.

"Leelee lied to you. She's been lying to you your whole life," Stella hissed. "And you shot her because you've always known that. Her black magic didn't keep you safe. It kept you prisoner. Only you were too stupid to figure it out."

Mr. Tobin clenched his teeth tight, dropped to his knees, and in a flash had the shotgun raised, ready to shoot. But Stella shot first. She'd had a pistol in the folds of her skirt. She shot straight and true. It was no accident that the bullet pierced Earl Tobin square in the heart.

Becky ducked, burying her head in Stephen's chest as she pulled him to her. His arms were limp, but they circled her, too, holding her close until the deafening silence made them both peek up just in time to see Mr. Tobin fall to his stomach. He dropped the shotgun and crawled on his hands and knees to Leelee's dead body.

Stella looked at Becky and Stephen. Without any expression on her face, she turned and went back into the house.

"Come on. Get up," Becky ordered Stephen. "We have to get out of here."

"My head is swimming," he groaned.

"Of course it is. You got conked on the noggin with the butt of a Winchester. You're lucky I'm here to help," she whispered.

"Am I? As I see it, you caused all this." Stephen got to his feet, but his knees were shaking beneath him.

"What? Let me tell you something, Buster. I didn't need a third wheel coming to glue up the works. I had a plan, and it didn't include you," she whispered. "Now come on. I don't want to be here when…"

Just then, Stella reappeared on the porch with a hammer in her hand. As she descended the steps, she began breaking every statue, jar, vase, and plaque that had been placed around and attached to the house, grunting and crying as she did so.

"What do we do?" Becky whispered to Stephen.

"I don't know."

"You leave," Stella said before turning around to face them. She sniffled and wiped her nose on the back of her hand. "There won't be any problems with your father's crops or your friend's family."

"Can we…do anything for you, Stella?"

For a few seconds, Stella stood there and looked at the ground. Then she looked up and shook her head.

"You witnessed a murder. If you feel the need to call the police, I understand. But know that I'll be leaving here once I finish this job. If they catch me, fine. Even in a jail cell, I'll be freer than I was in this house."

She went back to the task of shattering Leelee's trinkets and said nothing more to Becky and Stephen. The last thing Becky saw was Stella approaching the shed that held the two monstrosities with their mouths sewn shut. Stella held a match to it.

Without waiting any longer, the duo hobbled slowly into the darkness. The light from the burning shed could be seen deep inside the woods. Becky knew the two pitiful creatures that had been locked inside were no longer making noises.

"We'll call the police from your house," Stephen said.

"What? We're not calling the police," Becky answered calmly. "As far as I'm concerned, I didn't see anything. Didn't hear anything. Nope. And you'd be wise to dummy up as well."

"Becky, we saw a murder. Two if you want to be precise." He was obviously feeling better and getting the wind back in his sails.

"All right, tough guy. Say we call the police. What are you going to tell them? That we were trespassing on the property where there is a moonshine still and a bathtub gin racket going on? That doesn't look suspicious at all." Becky cleared her throat as they reached the tobacco field. "Then you'll have to elaborate on the fact that Mr. Tobin's maid tried to kill me because she thought I broke her mason jars. I'm sure they won't think we were sipping any of that hooch. Not a drop."

"Becky."

"Oh, and let's not forget that *my* parents, who are dear friends of *your* parents, will all be the topic of conversation at every gathering of two or more people from now until the Rapture. And even if they stick to the facts, which you know they won't, it will put both our family names in cahoots with the likes of Jesse James and Abraham Lincoln. Just remember that history may forget, but Southerners never do."

Becky propped Stephen up against the fence post as they approached the bald patch where the workers had pulled the sickly plants from the ground. On hands and knees, she felt around the stalks of the other plants.

"What are you doing?" Stephen asked.

"You want to mind your onions?"

"I'd like to know, since the last adventure you took me on *almost* got us killed," he retorted.

"*Almost* being the key word there. Aha! There you are, you little devil."

Becky's hands wrapped around the glass jar she'd seen earlier and pulled it from its hiding place. When she stood up, she dusted off her dress with her free hand. It didn't make much difference. She was filthy. Becky dashed the jar against another fence-post. Satisfied with it shattering into a thousand pieces, she went to Stephen, took his hand, and wrapped it around her shoulder in order to help get him to his car.

"I don't know if I can drive. My head is pounding." Stephen was putting more weight on Becky than he had been. He was pulling her closer and closer to him.

"Oh no you don't. You need to dangle. Beat it. Scram outta here. How in the world do you think it would look if you and I set foot in my parents' house at this ungodly hour looking the way we do? It's bad enough Daddy won't let me have my own boiler to drive around, all because of... well, that's another story. But if he sees us like this, all that razzle-dazzle in that smile of yours won't save you. He'll lay you out but good."

Becky huffed as they finally made it to Stephen's car.

"I'm telling you, Becky, I'm seeing stars. I can't drive," Stephen said as he leaned against his flivver.

In Becky's head, she argued and cussed and thought of a million reasons to send Stephen away. No matter what he said, his condition was not her fault. He'd brought it on himself.

"Okay, here's what we're going to do. But you need to follow my lead. No questions asked. Get in your car," Becky ordered but stopped Stephen short. "Wait, what are you doing?"

"I'm getting in my car," he snapped back.

"Not behind the wheel. You're hurt. Get in the back and lie down. Stick a leg out or something. Just scoot over."

Becky slipped behind the wheel, cranked the

engine, and hit the clutch and the gas, making the car lurch forward before it stopped short.

"Jeez, Becky! What are you trying to do?"

"Cheese it and sit back. And remember what I said. No questions asked."

With that, Becky hit the gas and sped up to the front of the Mackenzie home. She honked the horn loudly and called for her mother and father. Half the lights snapped on in an instant, and before she could figure out how to get the car to stop, Kitty and Judge were on the porch.

"What's going on?" Kitty cried. "Becky, my goodness! What happened?"

"Oh, Mama!" Becky cried as she climbed out of the car. "We got dry-gulched!"

"What? What does that mean?" Kitty asked, rushing up to her daughter.

"Stephen and I had decided to go to Willie's. Along the way, we stopped at a gin mill and then another, and Stephen said he needed some cigarettes. So we walked to the drugstore on Bryn Mawr on the way to Willie's, and some fakaloo artist—you know, a con—stumbled out of the alley and asked Stephen for a nickel."

"Oh my dear!" Kitty gasped.

Judge was busy helping Stephen out of the back

seat. Like a champ, Stephen groaned and kept repeating "Oh my head. My head."

"Well, Stephen, being the kind of swell egg he is, handed the guy a dime. Well, the ungrateful lout took out a sack of pennies and clobbered him in the head." Becky sniffed. "Then two more guys jumped out of the alley. We barely got out of there with our lives. We had to run for our very lives. And I ruined my dress."

"Oh my goodness. What is the world coming to? Judge, put Stephen in the spare bedroom. I'll get him some ice for his head." Kitty looked at Becky with worry. "Don't you worry about your dress. Mama will get you a new one."

Moxley and Lucretia were also up by this time.

Teeter, who was rubbing his eyes and yawning, held his mother's hand. "I want to know what happened to Miss Becky," he whined.

"Miss Becky's just fine. Let's go back to bed," Lucretia cooed.

"But I'm not tired," Teeter whined.

"Me neither. We'll stay up and count sheep," she continued as she led the boy back into the house to their room past the kitchen.

"Promise?" Teeter yawned again.

Moxley asked Judge if there was anything he

could do to help. Judge said that if he could scare up some extra nightclothes and a brandy, that would be most helpful. As Moxley turned to tend to Judge's request, he caught Becky's eye. She gave him a quick wink, at which he shook his head and chuckled.

"Oh, my! It sounds like a bomb's gone off." Fanny came stumbling out of her room with her hair in pins and tape over the space between her eyebrows.

"It's all right, Fanny. Just go on back to bed," Kitty said as she walked with Becky to her room.

"Why Becky, you look like something the cat dragged in."

"That'll do, Fanny," Kitty snapped.

"If you think I look bad, stick around. Stephen got the worst of it." Becky jerked her thumb behind her. Judge was bringing up the rear with his arm around Stephen as he led him to the spare room.

Fanny, fearing anyone might see her sans munitions, doubled back to her room and slammed the door.

It took about half an hour for things to calm down. After everyone got washed up and calmed down, Kitty and Judge went back to bed. Becky was tucked in tight, and Stephen was left in the spare room with a brandy and an ice pack for his head.

Within a quarter of an hour, Becky emerged

from her room and tiptoed to the spare room. Quietly, she rapped on the door.

"Who goes there?" Stephen whispered as he cracked the door open.

"It's me. Can I come in?" Becky replied.

"Oh, Fanny, I thought you'd never come," Stephen teased.

"A wise guy, huh?" Becky pushed the door open and slipped in. There was a candle burning on the nightstand. "We do have electricity here. Would you like me to put the light on for you?"

"No. It hurts my eyes. I'll be knocking off soon anyway. If Fanny doesn't come and pay me a visit, that is." Stephen smirked.

"I wouldn't be surprised," Becky whispered. She sat down on the edge of the bed while Stephen climbed in under the covers.

"That was some night," he said. His voice was so soft and light that the ticking of the grandfather clock downstairs almost drowned it out.

"I'll say." Becky rolled her eyes.

"That was some quick thinking on your part. Very creative." He pulled the blankets up around his chest and let his arms lie at his sides.

"Well, I had to explain that bump on your head and the state of my clothes. If you can't be sneaky about it, then go all in. That's what I say." Becky smiled. "You did pretty good yourself. I didn't need you to follow me. But I'm glad you were there to…be a fly in the ointment and cause me worry and…"

"You were worried about me?" Stephen sat up.

"I was worried about you the way a person worries about a feeble sibling or a three-legged dog. I was sure you'd be okay, but you'd probably slow me down." She chuckled before getting up from the bed. "How is your head?"

"It hurts. Can you hand me that compress? I left it on the davenport." Stephen pointed to the loveseat by the window.

Becky glided soundlessly back and forth across the room.

"Let me see?"

Stephen leaned forward and tenderly touched the spot that was sore. Gently, Becky placed the compress against the bump and eased him back against his pillow. But before she could pull away, Stephen grabbed her hand and pulled her toward him. Their lips met. Becky's heart raced. When she braced herself against his chest, she felt his heart pounding as well. Stephen pulled her closer and tighter. Had Becky not had her wits about her, she might have fallen into his arms and stayed there. But she didn't. She couldn't. Reluctantly, she pulled back from him. His eyes twinkled, and he smiled a sweet, innocent smile.

"I have to get back to my room," she said.

"Are you sure?" he said. "You could stay in here with me. We could talk about tonight. That was really something. If that's the kind of date you like to go on, I can hardly wait for our next one."

"That wasn't a date," Becky said, pulling her robe tighter around her waist.

"Sure it was."

"No, it wasn't. You were my chauffer for the night. And then you decided to be a party crasher. And now you're a masher."

"Why do I get the feeling that's what you like about me?" Stephen teased.

"I can assure you that I don't like anything about you, Stephen Penbroke." She slipped to the door. "But I am glad you're all right."

"Good night, Becky."

"Good night, Stephen."

Before Becky could slip back to her own room, she saw the shadow of Fanny's bedroom door close. Her cousin had been listening. It was not a surprise.

CHAPTER TWENTY-SIX

*I*t had been a week since Mr. Tobin had shot Leelee. In that time, it had made the local papers. Becky sat in her favorite red velvet chair as Fanny read the news article about it out loud.

"It says here that Mr. Tobin and his maid were killed by what the police say was a gang dispute over bootlegging territory. It also says Mr. Tobin's hired hand, a Mr. Edward Short, was found dead on the property from a blow to the head."

Becky had secretly wondered what had become of that Edward character. She let out a long sigh of relief, knowing she'd never see him again.

"Mrs. Tobin has not been found." Fanny shook

her head as she tossed the paper aside. "If she were smart, she'd run and hide for good. A woman with that kind of reputation would be wise to start over in a new town and maybe even change her name."

Becky remembered it had been right in this room that Hugh Loomis had made a similar comment about Fanny. Funny how people weren't really all that different.

"We don't know the whole story, Fanny," Becky said. "There are a lot of pieces to that puzzle, and I wouldn't even attempt to guess them."

"If you ask me, the land is cursed. Mr. Ruthmeyer's land and Mr. Tobin's land. If they manage to get a dollar for the lot of it at auction, they should be thankful," Fanny continued. "I wouldn't set foot on a square inch of it on a dare."

Just then, a loud horn honked, and a familiar jalopy appeared in the driveway.

"I don't think that Teddy knows how to arrive anywhere quietly," Kitty said as she looked up from her sewing.

Becky jumped out of her seat and ran to the front door. What she saw made her gasp and blush.

"We saw a friend of yours walking in this direction," Martha shouted, smiling as if she had just swallowed a gaggle of canaries. "It would have been terribly rude of us to not offer him a lift."

"Yes, Becky," Teddy replied. "He got all dudded just for you."

Becky cleared her throat and smoothed out her skirt. She opened the screen door and dashed down the front porch stairs before anyone could stop her.

"You look dandy as candy," she said, looking up into Adam's handsome face. It was as if he had joined the French Foreign Legion and had finally come home.

"Is your mama at home?" he asked in a low voice.

"She is. Maybe we should all pile back in the car and find a hash house for some grub and a Coca-Cola."

"Not just yet," Adam said and reached back into the car to grab a bouquet of simple, pretty flowers. "I'd like to introduce myself in a proper, Southern way."

"I don't know if it will make much of a difference," Becky insisted.

"Well, let's just see about that."

Teddy and Martha stomped up the steps like two elephants and went inside. Becky linked her arm through Adam's and escorted him in as well. When

Fanny saw Adam with Becky, she arched her right eyebrow suspiciously.

"Oh, Aunt Kitty. It looks like Becky wants you to meet somebody. How are you, Adam? Those are some lovely flowers," Fanny said, ruining Becky's introductions.

"Hello, Fanny," Adam said.

Squaring his shoulders, he walked past Becky's cousin and up to Kitty, who was watching with her eyes wide and a smirk on her lips.

"Mrs. Mackenzie, the other day I came calling on Becky, and I understand that it wasn't proper protocol to show up unannounced. I do appreciate your speaking with me earlier today and for inviting me over this evening. These are for you."

He handed her the pretty flowers, and stood straight as if he were saluting Old Glory.

"Well, that is mighty kind of you, Adam. I'm so glad you were able to make it." Kitty stood from her seat and looked at the faces of all the young people in her parlor. "These are beautiful. I'll go put them in some water and get Lucretia to make you all some of her sweet ambrosia."

Becky could have been knocked down with a feather. "You talked to Mama?"

"I happened to see her doing some shopping

today and introduced myself all over again. Plus, I did a little groveling. I think that helps." He tipped Becky's chin with his knuckle.

"Is this a mortuary, or are we going to put on some music?" Teddy asked.

"You know where everything is, Teddy. Go crank up that Victrola," Becky said while still staring up at Adam.

Within minutes, the house was filled with Paul Whiteman and his orchestra. Teddy and Martha wasted no time moving some of the furniture to make room for dancing. Fanny stood by the front door, her arms folded in front of her as she surveyed the situation.

"Don't worry, Fanny," Martha called out. "Teddy put the word out to a couple of his pals to join us. But don't play cards with them. They cheat."

"Martha, how is your mother feeling?" Becky asked. Since the day after Leelee had been killed, Martha's mother had made a miraculous recovery from the death sentence the doctor had given her.

"She's just ducky. That quack really had some nerve getting my father and me all riled up for nothing. He had her taking the big sleep already in a Chicago overcoat when all she had was a flu. Typhoid fever? That guy needed a head shrinker.

You can bet my father didn't let him off the hook easy, either." Martha nodded.

"I'm so glad," Becky said.

As if on cue, Judge came in the front door. He'd been out in the fields all afternoon.

"Hi, Daddy. Daddy. I'd like to introduce you to…"

"Adam White, I presume." Judge smiled politely and extended his hand to shake.

"Well, did everyone know you were coming over but me?" Becky huffed.

"Becky, had we told you, you would have been a nervous wreck all afternoon. You know she can be quite insufferable when she's on edge."

"Daddy, please." Becky rolled her eyes. "Don't listen to him, Adam. The tobacco goes right to his head and makes him loopy. By the way, how are the plants doing?"

"It's the strangest thing. Not a trace of that fungus on any of the other plants. I swear the boy and I checked every single plant in every row on every acre, and not a single speck on any of them. I'm grateful, don't get me wrong. But that sure was a strange occurrence." Judge scratched his head.

"Well, Daddy, you do have a way with things that sprout from the ground." Becky let out a sigh of relief. This was the good news she had been waiting for. It almost brought tears to her eyes.

As Judge excused himself, Adam pulled Becky aside.

"What's the matter?" he whispered.

"What? Oh, nothing. I guess I'm still shell-shocked over you making this special appearance in my house and sweet-talking my parents the way you have. That's a sneaky deal, Mr. White." Becky poked the tie that was hanging down his broad chest.

"That's not it. When your father was talking about his crops, you got choked up. I could see it in your face." Adam took her hands in his, and after looking to his left and then his right, making sure the coast was clear, he leaned in and kissed Becky's cheek.

Her heart skipped a beat, and her knees went weak.

"I've got a long story to tell you," Becky said. "But not tonight. Let's have fun tonight. Let's forget about tobacco and typhoid and even Mr. Gavin's rash, which has probably also cleared up."

"You're spinning some crazy yarns," Adam said.

"Isn't that the truth?" Becky laughed happily.

As soon as Lucretia appeared with a punch bowl of her sweet ambrosia, the party really started to swing. Teddy started a crazy game of charades just before a couple of his buddies and their gals came by. Two fellas who arrived stag quickly sashayed up to Fanny and were told every detail about the parties in Paris.

Becky and Adam danced the black bottom with lightning speed and precision, as if they were made to dance together. Fanny jumped in with one of Teddy's friends for a foxtrot while Judge set up the bar, bringing up the gin and champagne from the cellar.

It was a swell time. As Becky chatted and danced and took a seat extra close to Adam, more people started to arrive, until it was a regular Fourth of July celebration. It was after she'd finished her second champagne cocktail that Stephen Penbroke walked into the house looking dapper and sly with his parents behind him. Becky smiled and waved.

"Who is that?" Adam asked. He was sweating a little, making his hair curl across his forehead the way Becky liked it.

"That is Stephen Penbroke. Mama was trying to fit me for a set of handcuffs to that mug. But I think you have put a serious dent in her plans."

"Really?"

"Really." Becky stood up and yanked Adam to his feet. "Come on. Let's make with the introductions."

The boys were cordial to each other, shaking hands and quickly getting drinks. But it was obvious each knew what the other was thinking about Becky.

Not seeing any need for a fire extinguisher or a bull whip, Becky slipped outside to have a cigarette. After a few gulps of air and the caress of a cool breeze, she was about to head back inside when Adam appeared.

"It's hot in there," he said.

"Yeah," she replied.

"So, what's this story you have to tell me?" He stretched out his hand. She took hold, and they walked down the porch steps to a spot on the lawn just shy of the squares of light from the front door and the windows.

Becky stood so close to Adam he was practically looking straight down, but the smile never left his lips. She quietly told him about her adventure while inside, Stephen pretended not to watch from the window.

"Have you met Adam White?" Fanny asked.

"Hello, Fanny. Yes. We just met," Stephen replied.

"He's all wrong for Becky. She has a crush on him," Fanny continued.

"Sounds like you might, too." Stephen took a sip of his drink then looked at Fanny.

"And you're sweet on Becky. From where I'm standing, we might be able to help each other," Fanny said.

"What do you mean?"

"Well, I know where she goes, and I certainly know that her mother and father might be polite to him now, but he's a Northerner and from a questionable family. He could ruin her reputation." Fanny sipped her cocktail and batted her lashes at Stephen.

"Is this something you learned to do during your stay in Paris?" Stephen smirked.

"Maybe," Fanny said.

"So what's in it for you?" Stephen asked.

"Huh? Perhaps you don't see that tall drink of water out there, but I do." Fanny lifted her chin.

"Well, Miss Fanny. Maybe we should meet for a drink some time." Stephen clinked his glass to Fanny's, and they both took a sip. "Care to dance?"

"I'd love to," Fanny gushed.

Outside, the sun was setting on the tobacco crops as Becky continued to tell Adam about her dealings with Mr. Tobin and Leelee. Of course, his eyes were wide, and he begged her to never take such chances alone again, to which she crossed her heart and promised.

"Next time, I'll take you with me." Becky stood on her tip-toes.

Without saying another word, Adam took Becky's face gently in his rough hands and kissed her full on the lips, taking her breath away. The full moon was the only witness.

ABOUT THE AUTHOR

Harper Lin is a *USA TODAY* bestselling cozy mystery author.

When she's not reading or writing, she loves hiking, doing yoga, and hanging out with her family and friends.

For a complete list of her books by series, visit her website.

www.HarperLin.com

CPSIA information can be obtained
at www.ICGtesting.com
Printed in the USA
LVHW101751080723
751901LV00029B/356